DEADLY PLACEBO
An Adventure in Pseudoscience

by Christian Darkin

DEADLY PLACEBO

An Adventure In Pseudoscience
By Christian Darkin

Copyright 2020 By Christian Darkin
All rights reserved. This book or any portion thereof may not be reproduced or used in any manner whatsoever without the express written permission of the publisher except for the use of brief quotations in a book review.
978-1-9998930-2-6
First printing 2020
Rational Stories
www.RationalStories.com

For Rachel.

Chapter 1: An Invitation to a Glaring

Laura stared at the envelope. It was addressed, rather formally, to Christof Tourenski Mhp, PD, T, MNBA, FHsoc, AS, rather unnecessarily giving him his full medical title. Christof himself ignored the letter, and carried on with his breakfast as though he hadn't noticed it. Possibly, he hadn't. The Shatner's kitchen table was characteristically untidy and, along with multiple marmalades in varying stages of decay, it also featured a pile of books on psychology, a mobile phone battery, a broken sandwich toaster, several dead flies and an ornamental cake stand, currently being used to display beaded bangles.

Laura waved the envelope briefly at Christof. He raised his head, glanced at the address with a look of disdain, and returned to his breakfast bowl without comment. His mind was clearly elsewhere. She opened it for him, and scan read the contents. It was a request, and a pretty strange one, given the circumstances.

No, she thought. Christof Tourenski Mhp, PD, T, MNBA, FHsoc, ASD would not be giving a lecture at the Congress of Holistic Treatment Practitioners this year. And his lack of response to their emails had not been, as the letter suggested, because he was conducting intensive research, or off doing field work.

Christof Tourenski Mhp, PD, T, MNBA, FHsoc, ASD would not be attending the conference because Christof

Tourenski Mhp, PD, T, MNBA, FHsoc, ASD was a cat. And not a particularly clever cat either.

Christof Tourenski Mhp, PD, T, MNBA, FHsoc, ASD was a small, fluffy grey cat of unknown breeding and with one slightly torn ear. He had, as far as Laura could tell, no interest whatsoever in addressing a medical conference.

However, the arrival of the letter did mean one thing. It meant it was time to start solving Grandad's last puzzle.

Grandad had looked pretty serious when he had handed the cat over to her care, mind you, it was his last day alive - which would make anyone a bit humourless - but he had seemed to realise at the time that Christof was a pretty strange gift. He even looked her in the eye and apologised:

"I'm sorry I have to do this to you, "he had said, "just keep your head and you'll be fine."

The gift was strange for two reasons: Firstly, because Laura never really liked cats. Actually, that wasn't quite true. Laura liked cats in the same way that she liked giraffes: She found them beautiful. She respected their nobility. She wondered at their strangeness. But she saw no reason whatsoever why anyone would want one in their home.

And secondly, it was a strange gift because Laura's parents ran the Kennington Paws Cat Rescue Centre. Another cat was the absolute last thing Laura needed in her life. If she wanted to see cats (or indeed if she didn't) there were plenty of opportunities for her. One such, was today.

"It's going to be fine. It's going to be fine. Everything's going to be fine!" Judy said as she sailed through the kitchen, "and I'm sure you'll be ready to go soon!" Laura crunched on a piece of toast spread with the only marmalade on the table that wasn't either green with mold or worryingly fizzy.

Peter followed shortly afterwards - a shambling symphony in corduroy heading in the direction of "The Library". He stopped only to ruffle Christof's fur, "who's eating his breakfast?" he enquired with little need and even less response.

In fact, The Library, walled, as it was, by cluttered, dusty, overstocked bookshelves containing Peter's historical research work, would have deserved its name in any house but the Shatner's. Here, however, books formed a supporting structure in every room. If the bricks crumbled and the rafters rotted (which they might well do at any moment) the house would stand firmly on its skeleton of bookshelves. In fact, in Laura's house, the kitchen deserved the title "Library" as much as The Library did.

The only room containing no books was Laura's. Laura had a tablet. No books, no papers, no magazines, games, toys, ornaments, pot plants, beanbags, dreamcatchers, cuddly toys, chairs, desks or posters. She had a tablet, and a bed. It was the only place in the house with no distractions, and the only place which did not smell of cat. Laura had made sure Grandad had understood that her acceptance of his gift was on condition that the animal would never be allowed to enter her room.

Christof, however, had made no such agreement.

"We should try to get a little bit of a 'hurry up' on. Shouldn't we?" Peter called back to Laura at the breakfast table.

Laura decided she objected to the names "Judy" and "Peter" on grounds of economy. Judy had four letters. Peter had a wasteful five. Whereas the names she had been allowed to give them up to the age of twelve were not only more descriptive of their roles, but also shorter. There are, after all, only a total of six letters in the titles Mum and Dad.

Even years later, Laura hadn't been able to get used to calling them by their Christian names, but Judy had insisted, "Paternal titles propagate a hierarchical dependency structure which can be unhelpful" she had unhelpfully explained.

Laura realised, of course, that by her measure, Cat would have been much more economical than Christof Tourenski Mhp, PD, T, MNBA, FHsoc, but that was Grandad all over. Needlessly complicated.

She glanced at the letter again. Yes, it was time to start solving Grandad's mystery, but first, she would have to kill some cats...

By the time they had excavated the rubbish in the car and found enough seat space for all three of them to sit, they were already fifteen minutes late.

Peter started the car, and the stereo kicked in with his current favourite song. A few years ago, a hapless teenager had recorded a video for a dating site, in which she'd gone off on a tear-filled rant about how much she loved cats. Someone had taken that video and used autotune and a backbeat to turn it into a song. It had been a YouTube sensation, which had burned out months before Peter had encountered it and made it his unlikely driving anthem.

"... but I can't... Can't hug every cat..." spewed at cringing volume from the speakers and the car juddered out of the driveway.

"Are we wearing black today, Laura?" asked Judy.

"Yes," said Laura, "well, today I'm the executioner, aren't I?"

"Don't think of it like that," said Judy, "you'll see. It'll all be absolutely fine!"

Laura said nothing. Her parents were not idiots, but they could do a pretty good imitation of idiots when it suited them. It would not all be fine. There was no way on Earth it was all going to be fine. The writing was on the wall for Kennington Paws. Why couldn't they see that?

The car stereo rose to a crescendo, "... And I think about how many don't have a home...and how I should have them," Peter and Judy joined in, mimicking the autotune in just the way you would expect from a therapist and a university lecturer.

Laura's parents did not often come into contact with YouTube memes. They were largely unaware of the terabytes of Internet traffic dedicated to the cuteness of cats, and so when, from time to time, it did hit them, it hit them hard.

Chapter 2: Death Of A Hundred Cats

The car went quiet as they pulled up outside the sanctuary, and spotted the van in the driveway. White with the black logo on the side reading **NLFPC** – The National Legal Foundation for the Protection of Cats. The figure inside, hunched over his paperwork, didn't even look up. If Laura was the executioner, then this little man with his paperwork and his blue overalls was the fully paid-up, scythe carrying black-winged angel of death.

Peter smiled at him and knocked on his window.

"Would you like a cup of tea?" he said.

The man looked at him as though tea was a concept he had never heard of. Something so strange and alien that he couldn't imagine it existing in a rational universe. "I'm not ready for you yet. Please go about your business," he said.

For Laura, that business was working her way up and down the rows of cells, checking on each of the hundred and ten inmates. Changing litter, and water, putting down food. She could have done this later, but she was delaying her executioner job.

When Laura's parents walked the aisles and looked into the cells, what they saw were the cats. Sweet, hopeful little animals, each waiting for a good home, and, whatever their problems, temperament or ugliness, they saw each face as deserving of one. If the Shatners could only keep hold of each for long enough, then its ideal owner would come walking through the doors one day. Like gamblers, chasing that one big win, Laura's parents opened the doors each day with slightly desperate hope, and celebrated the little victories as they came, ignoring the bigger losses as they grew.

And that was all Peter and Judy saw. It was what Judy, if she had been any good at analysing herself, would have described as a "highly focused, subjective worldview". What Laura saw, and what the NLFPC inspector had clearly seen on his last visit was the squalor. The ground-in dirt in the corners of the pens. The old, wrecked toys. The torn and matted fur. The stale smell. And more than anything else, the overcrowding.

Peter and Judy were victims of their own success. They had started off by taking on a few cats and looking after them at home, but within months they had gained a reputation. Every cat that arrived prompted a flurry of publicity, and instead of using their interviews in the local press to say, "Thank you, we have enough cats now," they somehow managed to give the impression that they were a centre for re-homing every stray and unwanted kitten in the neighborhood.

Pretty soon, that was exactly what they became. They took on a vaguely suitable industrial unit just south of the river Thames, and organised a couple of charity events which, of course, drew even more publicity, and more cats. They got hold of some cages, and set up relationships with the local vets. They gained charity status, and everything went terribly well.

Laura liked the idea of her parents running an animal shelter. Building and decorating and choosing cat toys was fun, and it meant, for one thing that their actual house had fewer cats in it. However, Laura's parents didn't quite have her grasp of maths.

They realised, of course, that there were more animals arriving at their gates than there were leaving, but they saw this as a temporary thing. A blip, which would even out over time. They pointed out that they were finding homes for more cats than ever before. Laura saw it differently. She drew a graph plotting the five years of Kennington Paws as it became more popular. Cats housed against time. The number of cats being found homes was indeed rising. A straight line showed the growth in success.

However, when she drew the line showing the number of cats arriving, it was not a straight line. It was a curve, starting gradually, and then becoming steeper and steeper with every passing month. She had shown her parents how the gap was opening between the two lines, and warned them how quickly things would spiral out of control if nothing was done. They were not worried. They saw no reason why the curve should continue to rise, and in any case, they would cope until they could sort it out.

The curve did continue to rise, and coping became increasingly hard. Now they had over a hundred cats, and more appeared every day. They lacked the time, the money and the space to keep going. And while they dithered, conditions in the shelter were deteriorating. The visit from the NLFPC, and the grim reaper in the blue overalls was the end of their little fantasy.

By the time she had finished her rounds, the meeting had begun in the cramped office. Laura stood in the doorway and watched. Her parents had their backs to her, while the angel of death peered over his paperwork from behind the desk. She pictured his scythe leaning against the filing cabinet. Not a full-size scythe, of course. A little one for cats. Cute.

He was reading a litany of his parents' crimes. Cramped conditions. Several animals kept together in a cage. Insufficient ventilation. Untreated wounds. Contaminated water. It was like a health and safety report from a prisoner of-war-camp.

She could not see their faces, but read their body language from the back. Peter sat silently, absorbing every word. With each accusation, his shoulders fell a little further. Judy was bobbing her head around with mock surprise as though each charge had come completely out of nowhere.

"I hear what you're saying, "said Judy, "but I wonder whether you are externalising an internal discourse here. How would you describe your relationship with your mother?"

Blue Death wouldn't have noticed what the response was. He barely looked up from his sheets before continuing.

"We will be charging you with twenty six offences under the Animal Welfare act of 2006."

There was a silence. Laura had been expecting this since the surprise inspection a couple of months ago, but hearing it made it concrete. Peter made a sound like a punctured inflatable, and seemed to fold into his chair. Judy stood up and made some protest about "interactional discordancy."

Death himself seemed, if anything, embarrassed by the whole procedure. His job was, Laura supposed, not great fun for him. Most people got into animal protection because they liked animals. They hadn't really thought it through. She knew from experience that most of the job was actually about killing animals. Killing them, delaying their deaths for a little, deciding which got killed first, changing the manner of their deaths from, say a tumour to a lethal injection. Animal welfare was all, really, about death in one way or another.

The skeleton-faced bringer of doom, for example, probably joined the NLFPC out of love for all things small and fluffy. Yet what was his job now? To go around to homes run by well-meaning, desperate, overstretched animal lovers, catalogue the cruelty their underfunding inflicted on their inmates, break the hearts of those animal lovers, take away the poor creatures and put them to death.

Laura wasn't cynical about it. It was just one of those things. The only time it really bothered her was when her parents made her do it.

Judy noticed Laura hovering at the door, and whisked her out of the room in a showy display of motherly protection. "How can you do this in front of children?" her body language screamed at the man, who wasn't actually looking.

Laura quite understood the protective sentiment. She had felt it herself. Watching her parents being taken apart by this man, she had felt the urge to leap onto the desk in front of him, and hack him to death with his cat-sized scythe. And she'd have done it too, if the weapon hadn't been metaphorical.

At the door, Judy hastily fished in her pocket and handed Laura a book of stickers. Little round red stickers. The little round red stickers of life and death.

"Off you go," she said. Laura stared back at her. "Why not make it into a game?" Judy suggested.

The rules of the game were simple. The Welcome Animal Sanctuary in Brixton had agreed to take ten of the cats. Ten cats to be placed at their brand new facility, and take their place alongside the other inmates to get their shot at hooking a happy home. All Laura had to do was stick a red sticker against the name on the pen of each of the chosen animals.

13

Her decision would be final. Both in the sense that it would be her responsibility, and in the sense that it would represent the cats' last chance. This was it. The last lifeboat leaving the sinking ship. The final helicopter out of the city before the bombs started dropping. It was the red sticker, or the needle full of cold poison. Animal welfare, thought Laura, was a job best suited to psychopaths.

The first red sticker of life went to Neil Armstrong. His sweet little round face was impossible to ignore. Kim Kardashian got a sticker too - her attitude was docile and unassuming. She would make someone a good pet. Princess Anne was another matter. Her face disfigured in a road accident, she would win no prizes for beauty. Every so often, her jaw would fall out of its socket and get stuck at an odd angle until you clicked it back into place. Princess Anne would never find a home. Laura passed by her cage unable to look her in her one good eye.

Roland Rat fared no better, and Laura barely glanced at the Chuckle Brothers as she walked on by, condemning them to death. Nicolas Cage was alert and attentive as usual, his impossibly neat fur, and shining eyes catching hers as he paced. He looked like a dinner-suited aristocrat who had accidentally found himself in a rough prison. He was getting out, and he knew it, but somehow Laura couldn't bring herself to succumb to his arrogance. Besides, she could never forgive him for "Face Off". She walked on by.

A red sticker for Justin Bieber, and another for Boris Johnson. Nothing for the demure Jo Brand, or the impossibly sad looking puff-ball that was Vladimir Putin sitting fat and slow in the corner of his pen.

Laura would have so liked to have saved at least one of the celebrity chefs, but she knew none of them appealed to anyone but her. Nigella Lawson, Gordon Ramsey and Delia Smith all had such a zest for life - they'd have happily torn each other to pieces for a shot at the red sticker of life, but no new owner would have tolerated their spiky natures and wayward approach to toileting.

Finally, there was one sticker left, and one cage. In it, three cats: Marge Simpson - a fluffy ball of fun, Sherlock Holmes - dark, brooding and immaculate, and finally a tiny tabby kitten who had known no other life than the cage. Her title scrawled above the cage in Laura's own writing: "The Boston Strangler."

Her hand hovered over the nameplate. She could save Boston, but she would be condemning Marge and Sherlock. Could she do that? Boston would have a chance in the new sanctuary- an easy pick for some excited little girl. Marge was an old lady's cat, and enough of those came through the home's doors to guarantee her a quiet life eventually. And Sherlock - the deep, secret-minded cat of an arts student. He deserved to curl up on the still-warm keyboard of a laptop, and make his bed with the shredded remains unread lecture notes. How could she choose? How could she not?

She peeled the red sticker from its backing and held it over each name in turn. Impossible.

Finally, she crumpled the sticker in her fingers, and walked away along the long corridor of cages. Marge Simpson, Sherlock Holmes, and the Boston Strangler stared after her. For Laura, it was a kind of promise - a promise to all of them.

Either that, or she had just sentenced them all to death.

After the Pale Van Driver had pulled silently away, the Shatners acted immediately. Peter drove them all to the

Royal Tandoori, winner of the award for the third best Asian restaurant in South East London in 2006, for a celebratory meal.

The Shatners always had a celebration when things went particularly badly. It was a way, Judy always said, to take control of your own destiny. Neither her nor Peter mentioned the legal case. They discussed the menu at length - even though they always ordered the same set of dishes. They talked about Peter's work on Egyptian reincarnation myths. They even talked about the coming weekend, and Grandad's meticulously pre-planned funeral. They didn't mention the funeral itself, or Grandad. The fact that he was dead was completely ignored in vague exchanges about "The Weekend". To a casual listener, it might appear that "The Weekend" was a rambling holiday, or a weekend break to Butlins, but the fact that Judy's Father's funeral was mentioned at all was testament to the dark clouds that hung over the family. Laura joined in, but as her parents raised their glasses to toast the future, she leaned in and said:
"You do understand what's going to happen, don't you? You're going to have to make a choice."
"It'll be fine." Judy replied. "It'll all be fine!" She smiled a strange, forced smile. The kind of smile you might produce if you didn't want to make a fuss, but were being slowly swallowed by a snake.

Chapter 3: Grandad's Last Puzzle

Judy and Peter hadn't really understood why Laura had decided to bring Christof to the funeral, but Peter had defended her decision anyway.

"She just wants him to say goodbye," he had said, "Christof was his cat after all."

"I understand her emotional transference," said Judy, "But Christof doesn't want to be dragged across the country." She shifted her feet in the wastepaper basket that was the car's footwell.

"He doesn't mind," said Peter, "do you, Christof?"

"He looks carsick."

"He looks fine," Peter said.

He was sick - a little - but Laura quickly folded a napkin over it and wound down the windows to let out the smell, while her parents exchanged views on the cat's feelings in the front of the car.

They really didn't get it. This wasn't about Christof, or about her feelings. This was about Grandad. He was trying to say something by bequeathing her this cat, and perhaps there would be a clue at the funeral. Perhaps one of the mourners would recognise Christof from his past life before the sanctuary. Perhaps Grandad had trained the cat to - she didn't know - sniff out something at the lonely cliff-edge hotel which was the setting for the service.

As they pulled up outside the old, stone building leaning precariously over the cliffside, ivy curling up its walls, she caught herself - it was nonsense. Who ever heard of a sniffer cat? Cats did what they liked. Christof, doubly so.

They got out into a cold wind, and Laura hid Christof under her coat as they checked in. Her parents hadn't checked whether pets were allowed, and there was nowhere for them to go if they were asked to leave.

Having smuggled the cat up to their room, and settled in, Laura left her parents to unpack and smuggled him back out again to explore. The hotel was quaint. A little bit grand but not grand enough to call it a landmark. A little bit gothic, but not gothic enough to justify ghost stories. A little bit grubby, but not grubby enough to warrant a visit from the human equivalent of the NLFPC if there was such a thing.

It was, however, properly remote. It was central to precisely nothing, and Laura passed a generator and a rack of gas bottles around at the back. If they didn't have gas or electricity, then there was no point even checking if she could get Wi-Fi. The place was, in Peter's words, "a bugger to get to."

Once clear of the hotel, Laura fastened Christof into his harness, and attached the lead. Cats on leads were just a fact of life in the Shatner household. She had stopped feeling self-conscious about dragging a reluctant feline around the countryside a long time ago.

It was an odd, wild place for a funeral service, but it made sense. Grandad had grown up a little way down the coast, and he'd often spoken of seeing the place as a castle in the distance as he played on the beach. It had been a silhouette on the cliff-top, a place of symbolic mystery for him, and he'd spent his childhood making up stories about it.

When he'd grown up, inventing puzzles and mysteries had become his job. For thirty years, he'd set crosswords for newspapers, and devised puzzles for quiz-shows and parlour games. He'd become quite celebrated for it, and whenever anyone needed a particularly fiendish challenge, it was to Grandad that they came. His death had even been mentioned in The *Times* Obituaries.

But the thing about Grandad was that he was, at heart, a rationalist. He knew very well that the prize of solving a mystery was the game itself. The solution was never really the point. There was no real magic in the world, and the purpose of mystery was to allow us to believe, for a while, that there was. To solve a riddle was both the fun of it, and the death of it.

In his whole life, Grandad had never visited the hotel on the cliff. Laura understood why. It was because he wanted to preserve its mystery. Now that he was dead, he probably figured it would be OK.

Outside the hotel, there was too much wind to carry out her plan to stand on the cliff edge and stare pensively out to sea until everyone there realised that she was the dramatic heroine of a romantic Regency novel. Albeit one with a cat on a string. Instead, she cowered beside a fence and stared at the carpark.

Grandad had, she decided, made the right decision. She would follow his example, and never visit again.

Did her parents really think that everything would be fine? The NLFPC took no prisoners. Literally. They had no more room for the sanctuary's cats than the Shatners did. Her parents had two choices. They could bankrupt themselves fighting the court case, or they could quit, hand over the cats and see them put to sleep.

While Judy was packing for the trip, Laura had popped her head round the door of the library to ask Peter which books he wanted to bring. Her father was sitting behind his desk, head in hands, sobbing. There must at least be a part of him that knew the game was up.

In what sense was everything going to be fine?

Then it hit her. The problem was money. The cat home's conditions could be improved with just a little money, and possibly, the NLFPC could be persuaded to drop their case against them. This was the cornerstone of Peter and Judy's optimism.

Because there was a fair amount of money floating about in Laura's family. Grandad had a large house, and a fair bit of savings. Puzzles were a good living if you knew how to bait them with just the right degree of mystery and intrigue, and Grandad had never had much time for spending money because he was always too busy having fun. Grandad was clever in a way that meant he had not had to spend a second of his life doing anything he didn't want to do. Except the whole dying of cancer thing. On balance, he probably hadn't wanted to do that.

On the other side of the family was Granny Gryene. Peter's Mum. Granny Gryene owned a factory. Laura was not quite sure what the factory did. Something medical - but it was clear that it did whatever it was fairly well because Granny Gryene was always on planes to America and Europe and attending meetings across the world.

No, money wasn't in short supply in Laura's extended family. It was just that both Grandad and Granny Gryene were reluctant to let Peter and Judy get their hands on it. Laura had done enough maths on the Kennington Paws cats' home to understand their reluctance pretty well.

But now, Grandad was dead. After the funeral, Grandad's money would presumably fall in the direction of Judy, and "everything", in her words "would be fine." At least for a while.

Laura stared at the windswept car park. It wasn't conducive to thinking positive, beautiful thoughts about anyone or anything. That was probably why, when the square looking front of the dark grey car with the slightly tinted windows pulled up, and the thick-necked man with the dark suit and the immaculately cropped grey streaked hair got out, looked around and strode determinedly towards the hotel door, Laura felt uneasy.

Certainly, dark suits and grey hair were to be expected at a grandparent's funeral, and Grandad knew a lot of people from a lot of different worlds. Perhaps it was something about his body language that worried her. She watched him from the shadow of the fence as he stepped into the foyer and vanished from view.

Grandad's funeral was not conventional. The coffin was cardboard. There was no vicar, just a lady shifting nervously behind some flowers, while people stood up with unconnected tributes. The band was a nice touch, although they had probably played to more enthusiastic audiences. Nobody joined in with the chorus to "Happy" for example.

Laura looked around the mourners. They were a pretty odd bunch. Lots of them were younger than Grandad. Lots of media types. Newspaper people with suits that had been slept in. TV workers dressed entirely in black because black was the only colour clothes they owned. And here and there, the odd rescue cat.

Or rather, not the cats themselves, but their celebrity namesakes. Not big, world class celebrities with headscarves and minders, but the kind of people who did real stuff, and popped up because of it, on talk shows and documentaries. Two caught her eye. Sitting together at the back. Scientists. Melvin Rochester, the impressively eyebrowed elder statesman of chemistry, a man so committed to rational thinking that he'd virtually made a religion out of it. Next to him, Dr. Dan Pann the gangly rock star doctor who had become the go-to guy for any daytime TV programme that wanted to make intestinal tracts sound sexy and ridicule the latest fad diet.

Grandad had never mentioned them as friends, but then he'd never mentioned a lot of the people in the room. He'd certainly never mentioned the thick-necked man in the dark suit who was loitering unnoticed at the door. It wasn't clear whether the man was attending the funeral service or not. He simply stood at the door, peering in occasionally as though vaguely interested by the event, but not a part of it.

They had been Grandad's idea, the celebrity cat names. When he had come in to pick up Christof, Christof had been called Suki.

Grandad had said that cat names were an absurd human conceit. That a cat had no more use for a name than a chair did, and less interest in it. He pointed out that celebrity names had a similar pedigree. Nobody was born Minnie Driver or Eminem. A celebrity name was often the result of a committee meeting in which someone had decided that, for example, John Wayne sounded more like a tough guy than Marion Morrison.

Even when they weren't, they quickly became the name, not of a person, but of the image that person chose to project.

He had renamed Suki on the spot, and, while her parents were distracted, Laura and Grandad had spent a joyful hour renaming every cat in the home. Grandad felt that you should be free to change your name to suit the image you wanted to give out at the time.

It was even possible, bizarre though it may be, that Melvin Rochester and Dr. Dan didn't call Grandad "Grandad".

Of course, Christof was just Christof then. It was only in the later stages of Grandad's illness that the mysterious doctorates and titles started appearing after his name.

As the list of ad-hoc tributes began to dry up, the lady behind the flowers became increasingly unsettled. As though she wasn't quite comfortable with something on her order of service.

Laura half expected it to be Grandad suddenly sitting up out of the coffin and exclaiming, "ta-da!" or, more likely, running into the room shouting, "Pay attention: this is where it gets complicated," but he wouldn't be doing that. He'd already had a crack at the resurrection thing during that last long night at the hospital. Twice, his vital signs had dropped to flat lines on the screens. Twice the nurses had gently raised his hand and pronounced him dead with well-practiced sympathy. And twice, they had turned away only to have his breathing creak into life again, and his fingers curl weakly around Laura's hand.

It was a good attempt, and completely in keeping with his character, and his lifelong challenge to, "keep 'em guessing," but even Laura couldn't imagine him putting in a starring appearance at his own funeral.

She was wrong. One minute later, Grandad did something which was probably in very poor taste, but it made

Laura hoot with laughter. The flower lady shuffled backwards off stage, and Grandad walked out of the darkness at the back, and addressed the audience.

"Don't worry," he said, "I am quite dead." It wasn't a statement you'd expect a corpse to need to make at his own funeral, but Grandad had found a way to make it necessary, bless him.

He continued, "I'm being projected onto a film of cellophane across the stage by a projector in the ceiling." Now that he mentioned it, there was a slight glow to his body and a faded quality to his appearance. Ghostly was the appropriate word to describe Grandad for a range of reasons.

"I have been murdered," he said. He didn't have a particularly dramatic voice, but, it seemed to Laura that he made a pretty good attempt at it. "Some of you, here today, are my friends. Some of you are my family. Some of you are my killers, whether you know it or not, but know this;" he raised a finger and pointed. Laura felt a cold chill. It seemed he was pointing directly at her. Of course, because he was on film, and pointing at a camera, it would have appeared to everyone in the room that he was pointing directly at them. Nice touch, she thought.

"I am coming for you." he said.

The room was already utterly silent, so what went around it couldn't have been described as a hush. It was, thought Laura, a noisy sort of hush. A kind of un-hush made up of the sound of heads turning and glances being exchanged. Nobody spoke.

If you were to pick a particular ghost to liken Grandad to you'd have to choose Hamlet's father, who appeared to his son demanding revenge for his murder. Only Grandad didn't demand revenge, he politely requested it. And he didn't request it of his child (because Judy considered revenge unhelpful within an empathetic structure of reconciliation). He requested it of Laura.

"I wonder if you'd mind terribly avenging my death," he said, "I have been murdered, as I say, and I'd quite like to stop others from being murdered by the same people if that's all right with you." He didn't mention Laura by name and he was looking, of course, straight at everybody in the room, but she knew he must have meant her, and somehow, her cat, to be the tools of his revenge.

"Anyway," Grandad continued, "mustn't dwell on that, must we? Thanks everybody for coming." He reeled off a list of those present - singling out a few mourners for special thanks. It felt a bit like an Oscar acceptance speech - if stomach cancer was an academy award.

Eventually, he ended with a note to Laura's parents, "Oh, and a bit of an apology to Judy. For reasons that may, or may not become apparent later, there's no money for the cats. Sorry."

Either side of Laura, Judy and Peter visibly crumbled. Judy put her hand to her mouth to stifle a gasp, then pitched forward, eyes bulging as though she had been hit in the back by an arrow. She came to rest with her head between her knees. Peter just sagged as if all his bones had been removed. Peter did sagging very well. It was his primary method for communicating emotion. He could sag until his shoulders seemed level with his navel - and then just as he appeared to be done, he could sag again. Further, and deeper.

"Now, if you'll excuse me, I'm off to be reduced to ashes," said Grandad brightly. "Please stay here, and enjoy the buffet. I've made no arrangements for you at the crematorium. I've never had any fun at such places and I don't expect you would either. If it's nice, I'll pop back and invite you over. Bye now!" The figure on stage faded out slowly as he waved. A few people applauded, felt a bit silly, and stopped. They probably hadn't meant to clap, thought Laura, but if you work in the media it must be almost impossible to sit in an audience without pretending at the end that you had a delightful time.

Something had been nagging at Laura about Grandad's Oscar speech. As everybody shuffled out into the bar area where the buffet had been laid out, it occurred to her what it was. It was not who was included, but who had been left out. One person who really deserved a mention had been completely ignored.

When Laura found her, she was being harangued by Melvin Rochester. The angry scientist was pointing at her and talking rapidly in a rising tone. She didn't seem to be even listening to him. Her usually piercing eyes were staring back into the room they had just left, watching the coffin disappear slowly behind the stage.

Laura didn't stop to find out what the discussion was about. She stepped between them and stared Rochester straight in the eyes. "Leave my Granny alone!" she said.

Rochester stepped back. "I was simply pointing out - "he started.

"Zip it," said Laura. "This is a funeral."

Rochester paused, opened his mouth, took a breath, and seemed about to say something. At that moment, the nervous woman who had directed the funeral from behind the flower vase stepped up and whispered something in his ear.

"Excuse me!" he said shortly, and strode off with her into another room.

Laura turned to Granny Gryene who was still staring at where the coffin had been. "Are you OK?" Laura asked.

"My dear, I was just going to come and find you," she said, regaining her composure.

The term normally used in Laura's family to describe the relationship between Grandad and Granny Gryene was "as thick as thieves." Laura had thought, on more than one occasion, that they should marry each other and have done with it. They certainly had enough arguments to justify a wedding. They debated constantly at every family get-together. They behaved like an old married couple - which was exactly what they were - only not to each other. They were married, both of them, to long dead spouses that Laura could barely remember.

"What a silly man!" Granny Gryene said.

"Rochester?"

"Your Grandad! Just like him to show up at his own funeral!" she smiled. "Silly man."

"I was wondering," said Laura. "He didn't mention you in his speech?"

Granny Gryene sighed, "I don't know. We didn't talk much towards the end. As soon as he got worse, he just cut me off." She took a plate from the buffet and started to fill it. "I think perhaps he just didn't want me to see him when he was -" she struggled. Her plate was getting over-full now, but she kept piling food on it, "When he wasn't himself."

She looked at her plate. "I don't want all this," she said. Then she looked at Laura. "I thought he'd at least mention me," she said.

"What do you think about this 'murder' thing?" said Laura.

"Oh, just some of his silliness," she said. "He loved little games, didn't he?"

"Judy and Peter don't even want to talk about it," Laura said.

"You can call them Mum and Dad when you're with me," said Granny Gryene. "The thing you have to remember about my son is that he's not a clever man."

"He's a university professor!"

"Don't feel bad," said Granny Gryene. "Your Mum isn't the sharpest tool in the box either."

Laura tried a disapproving "You can't talk about my parents like that" look. Granny Gryene ignored it.

"Intelligence," Granny Gryene began, "is like a spinning gear. It can whizz round as fast as it likes - but if it's ever going to drive anything, it needs teeth."

Laura looked blankly at her.

"Your parents are intelligent," she said, "but they have no teeth."

"You didn't approve of their marriage then?"

"Good Lord! My dear," she said. "Of course I approved. Your parents' was an arranged marriage!"

Laura stared at her. "What do you mean? They told me they met at a university dinner."

Granny Gryene smiled. "One meets a lot of people at a lot of places in one's life" she said. "When your Grandad and I met - not my husband, that Grandad -"she gestured at the room where the flimsy cardboard coffin had previously stood, "it became clear very quickly that we were both clever people. I was good in business. He with his puzzles. It also became clear to us that we had failed to pass on our abilities to our children. We were not in love - far from it - but we did come to the view that if we arranged to bring your parents together, there might be a favourable outcome."

"What are you talking about?" said Laura. "What favourable outcome?"

"Why, you." she said simply. "Your Grandfather and I decided to conspire to create you. Our own children were simply the surrogates. Don't deny it. You have teeth, Laura." She picked a prawn from the buffet. "And when we get home, I think it's time I gave to give you something to bite on."

Granny Gryene smiled the sweet smile of a little old lady who ran a successful international company, and walked away.

At that moment, the hall doors flew open and Melvin Rochester strode out, closely followed by the usually chirpy Dr. Dan Pann. The two men were arguing furiously, but the moment they spotted Laura, they both clamped their mouths tight shut. Rochester's eyebrows shot upward, as if to mask his receding hairline. He looked like a headmaster who'd just been caught placing a whoopee cushion.

Clearly Laura's interjection had affected him more than she'd thought, because, after a second, he strode off out of the hotel. Dr. Dan stared like a cat caught in the headlights of an oncoming car for a second, then grinned reassuringly at her, and marched after Rochester.

Laura hung about around the buffet, pretending to be interested in the 1970s canapes, the cheese and pineapple hedgehogs, and the devilled eggs. She listened in on conversations for the rest of the evening, but heard nothing of importance. Most people seemed convinced that it had been a "lovely service." Laura decided that this was because saying anything else would be the equivalent of visiting a christening and mentioning how ugly the baby was.

Laura was particularly interested to hear what guests had to say about Grandad's ghostly apparition and accusation of murder, but all anyone seemed to want to talk about was *how* he'd made his appearance. It was a typical Grandad puzzle technique - give the audience an impressive looking, but simple trick to look at, and most people will ignore what you're really saying.

"Know your audience," he had always said. That was the key to manipulating them. And Grandad knew his audience. Every one of them.

Eventually, Judy decided that the time had come to call it a night. She had a headache, and proposed to lie down while the small green pills she kept on her constantly in case of such attacks took effect. Peter and Laura followed her up the stairs but as they reached their room, it occurred to Laura that the thick-necked man had been absent from the wake. Perhaps he hadn't been part of the funeral party after all. Perhaps he had just popped his head round the door to marvel at the low-level celebrities and the cardboard coffin, and the strangely animated dead man on the stage.

As they opened the door, Laura noticed something strange. Just next to the lock, a splintered dent in the wood had been freshly carved. It was as though someone had tried to force the big, heavy door with a crowbar.

Inside, the place looked as though it had been turned over. The contents of their suitcase were strewn randomly about the room as though thrown around in a panicked search. She smiled. It was exactly as the Shatners had left it. Whoever it was had clearly failed to gain entry. If someone had got in, they'd have tidied up.

She went to sleep with Christof curled up uncomfortably at the end of the bed.

In the morning, after a breakfast which was substantially better than the buffet, the guests began to thin out. Laura's parents were packing in silence in their room. Even Judy couldn't bring herself to protest that everything was going to be fine. Instead she concentrated on taking clothes which had, when properly folded, fitted perfectly well into their suitcase, and discovering that they no longer fitted when pounded back into the case in crumpled tatters. She paused only to glare at Peter, who alternated between flapping ineffectually around her, and sitting in a corner reading a book entitled "The Cult Of The Sphinx."

Laura took the cat for a walk. She could see the journey home would be more of the same, and she went looking for a less aggressive kind of silence along the cliffside road.

She let the lead out to its full length, and allowed Christof to explore.

The puzzle of Christof Tourenski was getting deeper. It was now, not just a puzzle, but a murder mystery. Grandad did have a taste for the grand gesture, so it probably wasn't an actual, physical murder. It would be more of a metaphorical thing. She had, after all, seen him die, and the moment had been distinctly lacking in smouldering guns, or phials of poison. His death had been exactly in keeping with his disease, and predicted well in advance by a whole range of independent health professionals, none of whom appeared to want him to die, or be doing anything to hasten his departure.

She was looking, then, for a symbolic murder, by an assailant who, Grandad seemed to think, didn't even know they'd committed it, but who might go on to do the same thing again, and the crime, if it were a crime, had something to do with a grey cat with one torn ear.

She was so engrossed in her thoughts that she did not see the car approaching from behind until it was too late. There was no pavement, so she was walking on the right of the road - closest to the cliff edge so that she could see any oncoming traffic and was not in the path of anything coming from behind. Christof had less awareness of road safety but he was walking at the end of his lead near the cliff edge, well off the road.

Suddenly, she heard the engine roar, and turned to see the huge square fronted shape of the dark grey car bearing down on her. She had a moment to recognise it as the car belonging to the thick necked-man in the dark suit, before it suddenly swerved - not away from her, back onto its own side of the road, but past her, and onto the verge next to the cliff edge.

The car was accelerating over the grass, and directly at Christof. The cat's legs scrabbled against the ground as it tried to bolt but it was at the end of his lead. Acting on instinct, Laura threw her end of the lead, and Christof scrambled out from the path of the hurtling car, leaping into the air, and straight over the cliff.

The car bumped back onto the road in front of her and sped off.

Laura ran to the edge and peered over. She wasn't sure what to expect - a tuft of hair stuck to a gorse bush - Christof floundering in the sea - cat jam on the rocks below? What she didn't expect was celebrity doctor Dan Pann grinning his trademark TV grin up from a path just below the ridge, holding the struggling cat in his arms.

"This must be the famous Christof Tourenski," he said. "Are you OK?"

"Were you following me?" asked Laura. "Anyway, he's not famous."

"Just out for a walk."

"Why was that man trying to kill my cat?" Laura demanded.

"I don't know." he said. "It's barely even starting yet."

"What is? You were following me!" said Laura.

"I'm just a humble physician," said Dr. Dan Pann. "Can I walk you back to the hotel?"

"If you like," she said, taking Christof and putting him on the ground again. They walked slowly back, staying off the road.

"You should watch yourself," said Dr. Dan.

"You think he'll be back?"

"When he realises Christof Tourenski is alive, yes, I should think so."

He paused, and took her hand. This was a man who had been on her television since she was ten. When she'd had her first period, she'd learned about it from him. "Your grandfather was a very clever man."

It was quite a statement coming from someone who, if he had a job description, it would read, "being a very clever man."

"I know," she said.

"-But he's playing a very dangerous game."

Laura thought about it. "Well, he's dead. If you can't play dangerous games then, when can you?"

"I can't tell you anything now," said Dr. Dan, "but here's my card." He handed her a printed business card bearing a large picture of his grinning face, "Call me if things get - well - weird." He looked down at Christof. "And keep your cat safe," he said, "Lives depend on it."

Chapter 4: The Real Christof Tourenski

In Laura's family, all the most important conversations took place under cover. Usually, the cover was some trivial topic which nobody ever needed to get upset about. For example, when the NLFPC had made their first inspection, Judy's anger and fear over the whole thing had been communicated through a discussion about washing up. Laura and Peter both recognised that Judy had never cared one way or another about which dishes were clean and which were dirty, or whether they were stacked in the cupboard or in the sink. So it was obvious from the moment she first mentioned how she wanted the family to move from a reactive to a proactive stance on the crockery cycle, that the visit had deeply upset her.

The language was clear enough, but now, in the car on the way back from the funeral, the conversation about the future of the cats' home was being conducted mainly using the medium of silence. Judy stared intensely out of the window. Peter glanced at her, and shrugged. Judy sighed at the GPS app on her phone. Peter squeezed her hand. Peter squinted at the road as though it had become shrouded in thick fog. Judy read a book.

It was a whole new language through which to discuss the black hole in the home's finances, and the impending legal action being taken out against it, and Laura couldn't help feeling it wasn't really up to the job.

However, the intensity of the debate taking place was far too great to allow her to concentrate on her own questions, so it wasn't until they got home that she was able to run to her quiet, empty bedroom, slam the door on the silent crashing chaos, and flip open her tablet.

There was a chance that Christof was somebody Grandad knew in his professional life. Maybe he had even been at the funeral - there were enough unknown faces there. Maybe Christof had been the thick-necked man with the grey hair - the attempted cat killer, trying to wipe out his feline namesake, for some reason.

That seemed unlikely, but Laura knew her grandfather well enough to avoid dismissing anything just on the basis that it was unlikely. Unlikely was Grandad's constant companion. Sherlock Holmes (the character, not the watchful, brooding cat) once said, "When you have eliminated the impossible, whatever remains, however improbable, must be the truth." With Grandad, it was quicker to start out with the improbable and cut out the middle man.

She typed into her search bar; "Who is 'Christof Tourenski'?"

There was not much.

Somehow, Laura wasn't expecting there to be. If there had been a selection of recent photos, and an interview on a chat-show about how much Christof enjoyed murdering old men, and running over cats, then she could have this whole thing wrapped up by teatime. But, that just wasn't Grandad's way. It was going to be bigger than that. Stranger than that.

A few suggestions for alternate spellings popped up, "Christchurch Touring sky", "Christening Turtle", "Chris

Toff Turandot", and a few random listings involving skiing holidays. Then, down at the bottom of the third page, "Christof Tourenski, Mindful Health Guru."

The link took her to a Wikipedia page. Christof Tourenski, it appeared, had had a colourful life.

Born in the former Yugoslavia in the late 70s, to highly religious parents, Tourenski had had a sheltered upbringing. An only child, he was educated at a small village school where he excelled in every field of learning. After a short stay in hospital following an injury sustained by attempting to scale the steeple of his local church, he developed a fascination with medicine, and when he left school, he went on to study the discipline at medical school in Kosovo. He quickly became the star student, impressing professors and fellow students alike with his phenomenal grasp of the science behind medicine. But he soon became famous in the institution for his impatience to be out in the "real world" helping patients.

His chance came all too soon when, just as his studies were reaching their end, and he was poised to pass with flying colours, war intervened. The Serbian army stormed the campus and the university was burned to the ground. The students and teachers were scattered, and Christof fled with thousands of his displaced countrymen, into the mountains.

He joined a guerrilla force and learned quickly to treat battlefield injuries among his companions, but his skills as a traditional doctor were not enough. With no access to medicines, he learned to make use of traditional herbal remedies. With no painkillers available, he quickly found other solutions, climbing to the misty peaks of mountains every night in order to study, by the light of the moon, books on hypnosis and acupuncture. He even once performed surgery, removing a bullet from a man's chest using a scalpel fashioned from a bottle of fruit brandy, and singing a traditional Balkan folk song to lull the man into a hypnotic trance.

His group fought bravely, but tragedy struck one day, when the make-shift hospital he had set up in the forest was accidentally bombed by a NATO strike force. Stumbling from the wreckage, Christof was the only survivor. Lost, and alone, he made his way through Macedonia, helping out with the Red Cross, and aid organisations, until he eventually joined a brigade of doctors in a humanitarian trip to the Horn of Africa.

Christof worked for two years in Somalia, training local doctors, as the country itself descended into civil war. He watched as US troops came through the country pursuing the War On Terror as they searched for those responsible for the 9/11 attacks, and as local gangs rose to fight it out in the streets for control of the lawless country.

And as he watched the unfolding disaster, he began to become disillusioned with his work. He began to realise that the orthodox medicine he was being asked to teach was of just as little use in the suburbs of Mogadishu as it had been in the mountains of Kosovo. He also started to realise that the locals had as much to teach him about medicine as they had to learn from him. He followed them into dark back-streets, and remote villages where he saw a different approach to healing the sick. He learned about the practices of shamanism, about the use of acacia bark, and frankincense.

He returned, stunned by what he had seen, but carried on his work. Then, one day a ship he was traveling on was hijacked by pirates, and Christof found himself dumped without food or water on the desert coast.

He wandered for days in the desert, surviving on berries and roots. Finally, when all had seemed lost, he sat down on a rock, and put himself into a meditative trance. He must have been just hours from death, but when he opened his eyes after what for him had appeared just seconds, he found himself in the centre of a bustling village, and seemingly in perfect health. It was four months later.

Christof emerged from his ordeal a completely different man. He resigned his work in Somalia immediately, and travelled to a Tibetan monastery where he spent a year studying the six yogas of Naropa, then promptly walked across the Himalayas to India.

Here, he travelled from town to town, learning of the healing powers of turmeric, and the homeopathic protocols of local clinics. He watched in awe as treatments handed down from generation to generation were used to cure patients of all manner of ailments.

At this point, the Wikipedia account became a little vague. It seemed that Christof had moved to the UK, and had become more and more reclusive. He had shut himself away for longer and longer periods of time in study and contemplation. He began to amass a huge library of medical journals, and would pour over them for hours at a time, absorbing their knowledge. He shut out the rest of the world, but continued to learn. Through correspondence courses, he began to attain qualifications in many areas of medicine (the exact areas of study were not mentioned). Christof had expressed a desire to return to practicing medicine, in the fields of research and teaching, bringing his skills and knowledge to a wider audience. But early last year, he had cut himself off completely from society. He was rarely heard from, and never seen in public. In short, Christof Tourenski had vanished.

By the time she had finished reading, Laura was beginning to see Christof as a bit of a hero. His name had started to become familiar. He was clearly a man you didn't forget. A man who deserved a wider audience. Perhaps she had heard of him before. Perhaps she had once seen a documentary, or read a magazine article. Christof Tourenski. Now that she thought about it, the name had a ring to it.

But what was he doing in the cat sanctuary? That was the question. She and Grandad had given the rest of the cats the names of relatively famous people. Christof perhaps deserved to be famous, but he was not. Something about all this did not ring true.

There again, Christof was the first cat to be named by Grandad. Perhaps he hadn't settled on the idea of giving all the cats celebrity names by then. Maybe Grandad had just plucked the name out of the air. Perhaps he'd been reading something about Christof Tourenski on his way to the cat sanctuary, and then decided, on the spur of the moment, that all the other cats deserved to be famous.

Maybe, there was a photo. She scrolled to the bottom of the screen. "Image of Christof Tourenski" was one of the links. She tapped it.

There was no photograph, just the black silhouette of a standard generic avatar. A dark head and shoulders outline, like Action Man on a witness protection programme. "No images available" read the caption.

No photo. That kind of a life. That kind of a profile, and no photo?

Then she read the note underneath:

Following the death of his parents, Christof became progressively more reclusive. Preferring to concentrate on his studies and research work, he removed himself from public life, speaking only occasionally at selected gatherings of his peers, and appearing in person rarely.

We, his friends await his return, and the impact on the world that return is certain to have.

"We, his friends"? Who were these friends? No contact numbers, no email addresses, no links. Just "we, his friends." It was a dead end.

Perhaps it wasn't Christof himself, perhaps the significance was in his qualifications. But the qualifications were just a few random letters. Googling MNBA or T. was pretty pointless. FHsoc revealed a number of options. The Forest Hill Society, the Forensic Homeopathic Society, an organisation for those interested in Ferret Handling, and an award for Flower based Healing. There were others, but Laura ignored them.

The following morning at breakfast, it became clear that Laura's parents had been doing something terrifying. Judging by Judy's dark, haunted eyes, and Peter's coffee-driven frantic energy, they had been doing it all night without a break. It was something they rarely did, and almost never to each other, and whenever they did do it, the results were horrific.

They had been talking.

Chapter 5: Peter With an Idea

Actually, 'breakfast' was not the right word. The mildewed marmalade had made the journey from what passed for the kitchen table to what passed for the lounge floor, and it had been joined by the remains of a bag of croissants which were both unpleasantly damp and strangely dry at the same time. There were no plates, and no knives. Laura held the croissant fragments in one hand and spread them with a coffee spoon which brought a dark, bitter undertone to the fizzy marmalade.

Judy sat cross-legged in the centre of the room, her knees just poking through a pile of scrawled, scribbled, and screwed-up paper. Peter circled the room, swooping and darting like a brown, crumpled vegetarian shark.

"Well?" said Laura.

"We can win. We can win!" Peter repeated.

"Peter has an idea," said Judy.

Peter with an idea was an entirely different animal from Peter without an idea. Peter without an idea was a shambling, shrugging, collapse of a man. Friendly, smiling and apparently unconcerned on the surface, but in a constant state of inner subsidence.

But, when he had an idea, Peter uncoiled. He grew noticeably taller. His arms and neck stretched. He still stooped, but now it was to fit his hugeness into the room. His hair reached outwards in tendrils from his skull. Most of all, his fingers stretched. They became part of his speech, fanning out when he spoke, and twisting around each other in gestures no human was ever meant to make.

Peter with an idea was a strange monster in constant motion. As though he was made of spiders. It was impossible to imagine one Peter while looking at the other - like trying to remember one song while listening to a different one.

Usually his idea was a concept for a book, or a piece of research. This time, Peter's idea was for a cat séance.

He delivered the idea as though it was the most reasonable thing in the world. After all, it had already run through the internal checks and balances inside his head, and so the possibility that anyone else might find the idea strange had been efficiently stripped away.

A cat séance. Peter elaborated: From ancient times, cats had been seen as supernatural creatures. Vessels for the spirits of the dead.

He began to list ancient cultural references - Egyptian Sphinxes, witches familiars, Mayan jaguar gods of the underworld. Laura cut him off before he could warm to his theme. She could hear one of his lectures coming on. Now was not the time. Never was the time.

"Ok," she said. "I get it. People think cats are magic."

Peter, it seemed, had once met, an animal psychic at a university event. A woman had proffered the theory that the dead often returned to guide their loved ones, in the form of pets. It was, she had told him fairly common for people to recognise their departed friends or family in the eyes of animals.

"I bet it is," said Laura, sarcastically.

"Do you see where I'm going?" said Peter.

"People are idiots?" Laura suggested.

That was not where he was going.

Judy took over, explaining that Peter's idea was to invite this self-styled psychic to host an event where audience members would be invited to meet some of the cats from Kennington Paws, and discover what bonds they felt. Judy described the event taking place in "an atmosphere of shared acceptance where no personal truths were off the table". Audience members would pay a small fee, and if they felt a bond with one of the animals they were introduced to, they would have the opportunity to adopt it.

In other words, Laura translated in her head, a chance to offload some cats and make a few bucks at the same time out of some recently bereaved loonies. Best of all, neither Peter nor Judy saw anything unethical about it.

Well, good for them, thought Laura.

The problem was that Peter's ideas were like the universe: they started as a single point of blinding light. But Laura knew too much to be deceived. The moment he began to speak about them, they exploded into stars and galaxies of expanding complexity. If you didn't stop him, an idea about toast could become a plan for global domination.

For the sake of humanity, it was necessary to freeze Peter's ideas at a reasonable level before they took flight, and somehow contain them. The only problem was that neither Laura, nor anyone else, had ever found a way to do that.

"... and that means we can raise the money to fight the court case," he said.

And this was where Peter's idea crossed the line. It went from absurdly funny to dangerously sinister. From the kind of clown you see pratfalling his way around a circus ring to the kind of clown that turns up in abandoned asylums with oddly shaped knives.

An evening of feline reincarnation might be entertaining. It might get rid of some cats. It might even turn a modest profit. What it wouldn't do was generate the tens of thousands needed to fight a court case against the most litigious animal rights organisation in the country. But with the decision made to fight the case, in Peter's head, there was simply no question. The balance of the money had to come from somewhere. And there was only one place it could come from.

"We're going to borrow it from The Account," announced Judy.

Laura felt as though she had been hit in the chest. Her mouth dropped open. This could not be happening. There had always been an agreement in the family - unspoken, of course - that the money in The Account was there for just one thing. Laura's university studies.

When it came time to pick a course, and it fairly soon would, that money would get her through whatever it was she decided to study.

Peter must have read her expression.

"We're only borrowing it." he said, "As soon as we win, we'll be awarded the costs, and we'll get it all back - "

But they would not win. Not a cat's chance in hell. They would lose, and her university fund would be gone.

"It'll be all right," said Judy, reassuringly.

"Oh, yes, another thing that will be 'all right'? Just saying it will be 'all right' will not make it all right!" She glared at Peter.

"This interaction is not helpful." said Judy.

"Shut up, Mum!" shouted Laura.

Peter looked bemused and hurt. As though he couldn't imagine where any of this was coming from.

"We're all making sacrifices," Judy said. Then she added, "If you'd shown a burning desire for any particular subject, then perhaps - but we don't even know what you're interested in studying."

"I don't know!" she balled at them. They both stared at her, blinking. It was the kind of stare cats gave when they were allowing you to think they understood what you were saying, but in reality didn't have a clue, because they were cats.

She threw the remainder of the marmalade-covered croissant onto the floor, where it would remain for some weeks, and stormed out of the house. She imagined the staring and blinking would carry on for some time after she left, but then her parents, like cats, would simply revert to their previous behaviour as if nothing had happened.

The sky was like bad rice pudding. Thick and lumpy and ready to drop in huge dollops onto the pavement, but the rain was the opposite. It was finer than sand. The sort of rain you couldn't see or feel, but soaked you all the same.

Laura walked through it in no particular direction. After a while, she realised she was looking for somewhere to scream. She didn't want the kind of little gasp of exasperation you could get away with in the street before ducking round a corner, but a proper outraged, yelling session of the type normally heard only in secure institutions.

There are very few places in London where you can safely scream. Even in the rain, it is a busy place, and even with its reputation for coldness, if you just stand and scream, someone will eventually interrupt you. Laura thought

Kennington Park would be empty, but dog walkers and alcoholics shared, it appeared, a particularly stubborn streak.

She tried the underpass, but, of course, the underpass was full of people sheltering. The streets were similarly sprinkled with rushing humans. The rain was not strong enough to justify umbrellas, so people generally opted for walking quickly with their heads sunk down into their coats. Laura walked slowly. She had nowhere to go, and even that attracted sideways stares from the collars of damp jackets. If she'd been screaming as well, that would probably have garnered too much attention. She took the back streets down towards the Thames. Victorian houses were rudely interrupted by 60s flats, with modern glass blocks sprouting through them as she approached the river.

Eventually, sitting on an iron bench watching the grey brown churning river failing to reflect the Houses Of Parliament on the opposite side, the front of her jeans getting slowly soaked, she gave up, and settled for her second choice of activity. Instead of screaming wildly into the rain, she decided to call Granny Gryene.

"They've stolen my university fund!" she yelled into the phone. At the other end, Granny Gryene, paused.

"Who's this?" Laura realised her voice must be unrecognisable. She hadn't even noticed she was crying, but she was. Not half-hearted crying, she was really, properly crying into the phone. She took a breath, and gabbled about how they were going to fight the hopeless court case. How they were going to 'borrow' her university fund to do it, and how they had no chance of ever getting it back. Granny Gryene listened.

Laura was struggling. Outrage and tears were falling over each other trying to escape her mouth, and her story came out in gulps and coughs. She wailed into the phone. Granny Gryene said nothing. Finally, she got to the part about Peter and his cat séance. Granny Gryene stopped her, and made her explain it again.

"Your father wants to talk to dead cats?" She asked.

"No, the cats aren't dead. The people are dead," spluttered Laura. "He wants to talk to dead people inside live cats."

There was a long silence. Then Granny Gryene started to laugh.

"He wants to -" She couldn't get the rest of the sentence out. Her sobs had turned to giggles. It was absurd. Ridiculous. Hearing it coming out of her own mouth, it was impossible not to laugh at it.

"Reincarnated cats!" laughed Granny Gryene.

"Shut up!" Laura giggled. "This is serious."

"Where are you, dear?" she said.

"Near Vauxhall Bridge"

"Stay there," she said. "I'm sending a car. I've got something I want you to see."

Chapter 6: Medicine Woman

It appeared to Laura, as she sat in the back of the hired car trying to dry her hair by shaking it through her wet hands, that the driver was taking the long route to Granny Gryene's factory. The landscape was getting increasingly industrial as they drove on. It was not the sort of place Granny Gryene's factory would be. This was the kind of area you'd expect *real* factories.

When Granny Gryene talked about her 'factory', the description was a little tongue-in-cheek. Laura had a picture in her head of a back room in a little shop somewhere, where ladies in cardigans packed boxes, and chatted about knitting while they wrote out addresses.

Granny Gryene's factory was never going to be some vast sprawling industrial complex full of boiler-suited workers fussing over giant, incomprehensible machines with dials and pipes all over them. That just wasn't her style.

However, it appeared the driver was taking her on a tour of a few vast sprawling industrial complexes first. Either side of the road, industrial units were bustling with activity. It was not like the industrial estate where The Kennington Paws Cat Sanctuary struggled by, squeezed in among the web-designers, and the garages.

"Where is Gryene's?" She asked the driver as they drove down the row of white buildings, past the queues of articulated lorries being loaded with shrink-wrapped pallets. He looked back at her in the rear view mirror.

"It's all Gryene's," he said simply. Laura looked around. That couldn't be right!

They pulled up outside the factory's main reception. Granny Gryene was waiting for her. Dressed in a smart blue suit and with her hair tied up, she looked younger. Granny Gryene smiled, and hugged her, but somehow, it wasn't right. Not the familiar hug she gave out when she visited Laura at home. It was a hug with reservations. The kind of hug you give someone you've just met. A hug that said, "From today, things are going to be different."

"Welcome to Gryene's," she said.

She led Laura through reception - a large white room which felt both welcoming and at the same time, vaguely surgical. As though it were the waiting room for a plastic surgery clinic. There were expensive leather sofas arranged around a glass coffee table. On the table, a book featuring Victorian watercolour paintings of plants and flowers lay open and unread. A water feature stood against one wall - a metal ball with water trickling out of the top, and flowing down between grey pebbles at the bottom. Above it, a large plasma screen showed an image of a green-masked scientist dripping blue liquid one drop at a time into a huge tank of water. Each drop exploded into clouds of colour, before dissipating into nothing.

"What do you do here?" Laura asked.

"Let's start at the beginning, shall we?" She led Laura through a set of double doors and onto the factory floor. Laura looked around. It was like Willy Wonka's chocolate factory. Only instead of a river of chocolate, there was a conveyer shuffling an endless stream of pills. Brightly coloured, and moulded into different shapes and sizes, they poured along pipes, over falls, and down chutes. Just as in

Willy Wonka's factory, they looked like sweets, and just as there, you felt that bad things would happen if you ate them.

"You make pills?" said Laura. "You're a medicine factory?"

"We make naturopathic remedies," she explained. "Vitamin pills." She pointed at a conveyer of lozenge shaped pills in muted shades of green and brown. "Manuka honey, and grapefruit seed extracts." She gestured to a vat of glassy yellow capsules which seemed to be made from captured sunlight. "Flower remedies, natural supplements, herbal concentrates. But our bestselling range is our homeopathic treatments. All completely natural, and organic."

Laura looked at her. She didn't have a clue what Granny Gryene was talking about. For Laura, medicine was something you were given when you were ill. You shut your eyes, and took it. At some point later you got better. There was, she had allowed her mother, and various doctors to convince her, some kind of connection between taking the medicine and getting better. That was apparently part of the deal. Unless you were Grandad. If you were Grandad, you took the medicine, and you didn't get better. You got worse, and then you died.

As far as medicine was concerned that was pretty much all Laura knew, and until she had done her research on Christof Tourenski, it was all she had wanted to know. Granny Gryene, it appeared, knew an awful lot more.

"What do they do?" asked Laura.

"We manufacture the remedies. Prescribing naturopathic medicine is a very individual process. It's one of the differences between us and conventional medicines - you see, each person is different. Giving everyone the same treatment just because they've got the same symptoms is just ridiculous.

That's what a conventional doctor would do." She somehow made the phrase, "conventional doctor" sound like the phrase "six-year-old with a toy stethoscope".

At the far end of the room, a huge machine like a cement mixer was churning about a million round, green pills. Laura recognised them as her mother's headache tablets. A man in a loose fitting plastic all-in-one was spraying the pills with a fine mist of liquid. He looked like a baggy jelly baby.

"What's he doing?" asked Laura.

"The homeopathic pills start off with nothing in them. We call them 'blanks'" She pointed to a vat of pills on the other side of the factory. "He's adding the active ingredient," Granny Gryene said, "It's highly potent."

"Is it safe to stand here?" Laura asked.

"Of course," said Granny Gryene. "There are no side effects with these medicines." Laura thought of Grandad and how sick his medication had made him towards the end.

"I thought all medicines had side effects," she said.

"Not these," said Granny Gryene. "The side effects come from the chemicals," she smiled.

They stood and looked into the slowly tumbling sea of green pills. They churned and flowed. There was something hypnotic about a million tiny, identical things moving as one. Like gazing at the atoms of the universe, or watching commuters file through a tube station.

Granny Gryene turned slowly to look at Laura. She started to giggle.

"Cat séances!" she said. Laura smiled. Then laughed. Soon, they were both doubled up, helpless with laughter. A man with a clipboard appeared, and waited patiently beside them until Granny Gryene had regained herself enough to sign a paper. Then he hurried away.

"Come on," said Granny Gryene. "Let me show you the rest."

They walked through the factory. Past the packaging machines, separating each pill, and wrapping it into plastic bubbles, or pouring them to precisely fill little bottles. Past the labelling and boxing stations where every product was stamped and stuck with perfectly fitting printed labels and tiny boxes. Dextrous mechanical fingers placed and arranged each box of medications, and marked it for dispatch to addresses all over the world.

They walked through the homeopathic lab where scientists in sterile gloves and masks worked with dark and tiny bottles of coloured liquids, and huge jars of pure water. Precise electronic scales, and machines designed to vibrate, spin and minutely examine solutions sat in racks. Granny Gryene explained little details as they passed. It was all tightly controlled. Precise. Perfect. In one room, Laura saw purple flowers soaking in a vat of water. In another, she glimpsed a row of leather pads and next to each, a scientist holding a big solid jar of what looked like pure water. In turn, each scientist raised up their jar, and brought it down on the pad in front of them in an exactly measured impact.

Every time they stopped at a machine, someone wanted to talk to Granny Gryene about something urgent. Every time they walked down a corridor, people would fly out of offices to ask questions or get her to sign documents. Granny Gryene's phone rang. She answered it immediately. "No, I can't deal with that now," she snapped, and switched the phone to silent.

"This is my office." Granny Gryene ushered her inside. "Hold all calls!" she shouted into the corridor as the door clicked shut. Granny Gryene's office was not like the rest of the factory. Her desk was a mess of papers, and phones. A computer screen sat in the corner. It appeared to be mainly used as a storage medium for post-it notes, and looked like it needed replacing with something that didn't run on steam.

Granny Gryene sank into a chair and in that moment, the Willy Wonka act was gone. Suddenly, she looked exhausted. Old. And there was a look in her eyes. It was a look she recognised instantly. Her father had it. Her mother had it. The exhaustion. The desperation. The hopeless struggling on.

It might have looked like a shiny, new industrial complex, operating like a well-oiled machine, but in reality, it was just like the cat sanctuary, and Granny Gryene was a woman on the edge.

"You've grown too fast," said Laura simply, "your business got more and more popular, bigger and bigger, and you just weren't ready for it. Now you can't cope."

Granny Gryene smiled, but there were tears in her eyes, "I've got a board of managers with years of experience in this industry. I've got independent consultants, and advisors and even a social media engagement enabler, whatever the hell that is," she paused. "And none of them can see it. And it took you fifteen minutes."

Laura shrugged. "What are you going to do?"

"That depends on you," she said. Laura looked at her.

"What are you talking about?"

"I want you to take over." Laura sat back in her chair. That came out of nowhere. Was she serious? Laura looked at her. She was serious. Serious. Desperate. Frail.

"Me? But I'm still at school. And I don't know anything about this stuff!"

Two good points Laura thought, but Granny Gryene was unpersuaded: "Not now. I want you to train. I'm offering to fund your education."

Laura's mind was racing. Until today, Laura's granny was, well, a granny. She was always a formidable granny, and one with a sharp mind. But now, in her business suit, sitting behind her desk at the head of the kind of business empire you'd expect from a James Bond villain, Laura felt her perception shifting. It was like that moment when, staring at an optical illusion, you suddenly realise that what you thought was a picture of Marilyn Monroe was really an image of Albert Einstein. The two images of Granny Gryene hovered in her brain, fighting for control. The woman in front of her changed from one person to another, and back before her eyes.

She looked up at the wall behind Granny Gryene. Diplomas dotted the wall. Her eyes focused on one right in the centre. Her mouth dropped open, "Granny Gryene- " she started.

"Sylvia. Here, my name is Sylvia."

"Sylvia -" The name was right. This was a different woman from Granny Gryene. A different relationship. It wasn't like calling Judy, Judy instead of Mum. This was a proper mark of respect. "What is that?" Laura pointed. The framed certificate read, "MBNA"

Sylvia looked round, "That's my diploma in Natural Alternative therapies. It's a tough course, but I'm willing to put you forward."

"I know," said Laura. "My cat has one." Sylvia looked puzzled. Laura smiled as though it were a joke.

"You don't have to decide now," said Sylvia," Go home. Have a think about it, and then make your decision. I'll have my driver take you."

They drove back through the industrial complex. The rain was thicker now, blurring the view through the windows. She sat in the back of the car, and looked out. That lorry, she thought, mine. That building. That gate. That strange, incomprehensible tangle of machinery and pipes, whatever it did. Mine. Her grandmother's office. Her responsibilities. Her life. One day.

But right now, Christof's diploma. That same qualification the mysterious battlefield medical guru had studied for could be hers. Her two new heroes, Christof and Granny Gryene had chosen the same qualification to study for. That was some endorsement.

Maybe that was what Grandad was trying to say by giving her the cat. Maybe he was giving her a direction.

Maybe.

The car rolled on.

Chapter 7: The Dead Cat People

There is an internationally recognised set of conditions which you must meet before attempting to contact the dead. Laura had seen enough films, and read enough books to know this.

Graveyards were good. Old, ruined churches were better. Candles were essential - unless you could procure an unearthly green glow which appeared to emanate from nowhere. Icy mist wafting slowly across the floor would be handy. Eccentric elderly ladies with flowing dresses and absurd hair, making incomprehensible noises in strange accents as they glared off into the distance were a given.

However, in the case of her parents' cat séance, a combination of thrift, lack of imagination, and health & safety rules conspired to dampen the atmosphere.

The vicar of the old, gothic church at the end of the street had rejected the séance on religious grounds - worried, Laura assumed, that one of the cats might host the spirit of some ancient demon. Judy had access, through her therapy sessions, to a range of meeting rooms which would have been ideal if they had been hosting a self-help group. As it was, the community centre felt that the presence of so many cats in a small place might present an allergy risk, that candles would be banned because of fire insurance, and that the question of whether cats had souls would need to be debated by several interfaith committees before it could be decided whether it was offensive to anyone.

Peter had more success with his university. Laura could imagine him pointing with his spidery fingers at the board as he expounded his ideas at them in bewildering and expanding detail. "No," they would have said, and he wouldn't even have drawn breath. "No," they would have repeated as he unpacked the arguments one by one. "No?" They would have protested as he turned their every objection into a compelling reason why a cat séance was the only viable way forward for their organisation.

Somewhere in the conversation, it would have become apparent that each "No" just forced Peter to make his plan bigger, and that letting him do what he wanted to do would be the easiest course. They were probably still saying "No," even as they signed the documents allowing Peter to use the faculty's little theatre space for his project.

Laura looked around it. Not perfect. The stage was already set up for the university's next production; a traditional comic farce involving bigamy, vicars and hilarious mistaken identities, but re-interpreted as modern dance. The séance would have to take place in a badly constructed surreal version of a 1970's living room. While her parents fussed around with paperwork, and cat food, Laura set to work trying to salvage the atmosphere. This was important. The event was absurd, and hopeless, but unless it worked, and worked spectacularly, the money for Laura's education, not to say everything else they owned, would go in court costs.

Laura had already made a start on the maths. She'd worked up a quick spreadsheet on her phone. Costs of the event, entry price, court costs. Estimates, of course, but she always felt safer when she had a number in her head. Besides, as the real numbers started to appear, she would be able to fill them in on her spreadsheet and the result would get closer and closer to reality.

By changing the values in all the fields, and setting up some basic formulae, important values were calculated: entry price multiplied by size of audience minus costs equals profit. Lawyers' fees multiplied by parental stubbornness equals court costs. Court costs minus profit equals Laura's education fund destruction.

Size of audience multiplied by audience gullibility equals number of cats offloaded to people who thought they were taking home their dead relatives. That figure taken away from number of cats in the sanctuary equals Dead Cat Quotient.

This last figure was key. One day, probably quite soon, Laura would have to walk into the sanctuary with a vet, and one at a time, she would have to hold down each cat while it was put to death. Her parents would not be able to bear to be there on Dead Cat Day. It would just be her and the vet.

In years to come, Laura was fairly sure she'd be sitting in a therapist's office talking through Dead Cat Day. She would be re-living it in every heart shredding detail for the rest of her adult life. Laura didn't want cats in her life, but she did not want dead cats on her conscience either.

Getting the Dead Cat Quotient as low as possible had to be her aim. If nothing else, it would reduce her therapy bills in the future.

It was, at least, possible to make the theatre atmospherically dark. She fiddled around with the lighting desk until she found something suitably sinister. A dim green and red glow with a spotlight on the centre table. Then she went down to the cafe outside the theatre. This was where the crowds of mad cat people would be beginning to gather.

She'd be able to take a sample of the numbers and make a guess for her spreadsheet.

There was nobody. The drips from the unused coffee machine as it waited in vain to churn out cappuccinos were the only sound. Her parents had been emailing and putting up posters frantically. There had even been a piece on local radio, but clearly, the message that the supernatural event of the decade was taking place, simply hadn't got through.

Laura sat down, and waited. She tapped "MBNA Natural Therapy" into Google, and was rewarded by a website of densely packed, technical looking text and diagrams interspaced with photos of water droplets and flowers. This was going to require some looking into, but if Granny Gryene and Christof had both got through the course, she would give it her best shot. Further down, she noticed there were options on different ways to take the course - "self-study" was apparently an option, whatever that meant.

Swiping back to the search results list, Laura scanned down it. The qualification looked as though it was pretty well regarded - aside from some predictably dismissive rants about it from the likes of Melvin Rochester. She turned off her phone. This stuff would have to wait. The one ray of hope in the whole dismal cat séance debacle had just materialised in the cafe: Ms. Blythe, the animal psychic.

Ms. Blythe had obviously read all the same books, and seen all the same films as Laura. She had observed the characteristics of the batty, wild eyed psychic medium cat lady, and she had absolutely nailed the part.

The moment she strode into the room, looking like a pantomime gypsy, she dominated.

"Darling, I sense great skepticism in you," she said, gripping Laura by both hands. No kidding, she thought. "Is this your cat?"

Christof Tourenski was winding his leash around Laura's feet, binding her to the spot.

"No, he's my Grandad's,"

"I think he is your cat," she said. Then she paused in what she probably hoped was a mysterious way, "Cats have much to teach us, you know."

"Well, he does have several degrees," said Laura seriously. Ms. Blythe looked puzzled.

"I think you two have a long way to travel together."

"Save it for the audience," snapped Laura, irritably. "They're waiting for you backstage."

Half an hour later, everything was prepared.

Peter was buzzing, backstage among a pile of cats. The celebrity chefs were hissing at each other from their cages. The Boston Strangler played quietly in a corner. Sherlock paced, back and forth, the same motion repeated over and over, endlessly watching. Nicolas Cage was still, preened, ready. Behind his eyes, he seemed to be preparing for his performance.

"It's time," said Laura.

"You could start letting them in, couldn't you?" said Peter.

"I don't think we'll need to barricade the doors," she said sarcastically. "There was no one in the cafe." She wandered off towards the theatre doors.

A few minutes later, Laura put her head around the curtain and called out to Peter; "What do we do with the people who won't fit in the theatre?" she said. "There are about two hundred more than will fit."

Peter smiled. "I've had video screens put up in the conference room."

"You were expecting this?" Laura was amazed.

"People like cats," said Peter simply.

Bathed in her green and red light, Ms. Blythe kicked off her address by trying to gauge her audience: "Does anybody have direct experience of a loved one returning to this plane in the form of a cat?" Impossibly, Ms. Blythe pulled off a tone of voice which suggested, not only that this was a perfectly reasonable question, but also that she genuinely cared about the answer.

Then something even more incredible happened. One by one, hands started to go up in the audience. Laura stared out from backstage. The showmanship of this strange little woman was amazing. She certainly knew how to work her audience.

The first lady to get to her feet was in her eighties, but her voice was piercingly clear as she described how she had lost her husband some years before. Her voice did not vary as she spoke of how he had choked to death one day on his favourite homemade Battenberg cake. She spoke with utter confidence as though she was reading excerpts from another person's life as she outlined the paralysing loneliness she had felt. She had, she said, carried on tending their garden throughout the summer, and she had sat outside every morning at eleven, with a cup of Earl Grey tea. She had poured a cup for him, and laid out a Battenberg on a folded doily by his favourite garden chair, despite the fact she hated the stuff herself.

Her voice began to falter as she continued. One day, a stray cat had appeared in the garden, its hair the same colour as her husband's, its eyebrows as dark and heavy as his, her voice began to falter. The cat had not hesitated. Tt had hopped straight onto the table, taken a bite out of the Battenberg, licked Earl Grey tea from the bone china cup, and then sat back in her husband's old chair. At this point, the lady paused. She knew what she was saying was impossible. The cat, she said, had looked straight at her, its eyes wide and understanding. In that moment, she had known that this was her husband, returned to her side. In the years that had passed since, she had not had a second of doubt.

The pink-haired, nose pierced girl in the dungarees who stood up next, went on at great length, jumping from one subject to another. She talked about her life, and her quest to explore the shared condition of humanity. She mentioned spiritual dimensions, and guardian angels. She spoke of her cat, and of her ex-boyfriend interchangeably, so it wasn't quite clear to Laura which had followed her around all day, peering over her shoulder, and which had the rough tongue and grey whiskers.

By the end of her speech, for which Ms. Blythe thanked her deeply, it was very clear this strange girl felt that the cat was the spirit of her ex-boyfriend, returned to look over her. It was a charming notion, thought Laura, but the girl had never explicitly said that the ex-boyfriend was dead. Laura wasn't sure if you could be reincarnated while you were still alive. It seemed to raise philosophical questions she didn't feel qualified to answer - especially since the whole thing was plainly nonsense.

Nonsense or not, the audience were enraptured. It was as though Ms. Blythe had tapped into something they all, in their hearts, already knew, but that they had all thought nobody else in the world had recognised. By the time the third speaker had sat down, there was a warm glow coming from the audience. They had, it seemed, all shared a deep revelation about the nature of the universe. It was something strange, and beautiful. Something life-changing, and something which, once shared, bound these strange individuals together with an invisible cord.

When Ms. Blythe signaled for Laura to bring forth the first of the feline spirits, she noticed the whole audience leaning forward, squinting into the deep green and red light to see which cat she was holding.

"What," asked Ms. Blythe, raising a hand to the heavens, "is his name?"

Laura opened her mouth to introduce Nicolas Cage to the rapt audience, then realised Ms. Blythe was not asking her. Nicolas Cage struggled from her hands, onto the table. He raised his head to the audience and stared out. Ever the performer, Nicolas owned the stage as he slowly paced up and down the table, staring out as though looking for something or someone in the crowd.

"Roger!" a voice from the back of the room burst out, seeming to surprise itself. The owner of the voice gasped as though he had not meant to speak, then whispered hesitantly again. "Roger?"

All eyes turned to a mature man in a purple cravat. He was old enough to know better, but he plainly did not. The man stood up, and navigated his way to the stage, his gaze fixed on the cat. By the time he reached the front, his eyes were wet. He blinked and a single tear rolled down his cheek.

He started to speak, but the only sound he made was a sob. Visibly shaking, he gathered the cat up in his arms, and Laura ushered him safely backstage.

Laura watched as he held Roger to his face. The cat was Roger now. Nicolas Cage was gone. There was not a trace of him. It was as though he had taken his face off.

Grandad was right. Names outlived their usefulness.

Peter and Judy must have really gone to town, thought Laura. They had dug deep into the strata of Peter's rarified academic life, and Judy's therapy work, and they had unearthed an unearthly audience. They had mined a rich seam of strange, mad, impressionable souls.

Alone, these people were strange curiosities. The sort of people you would notice in the street, but not remark on. He, or she is odd, you would think, without even being aware that you were thinking it. The tall, prim lady sitting alone with her Earl Grey tea at the same time every morning. The weird, spaced-out girl with the pink hair seeing fairies at the end of the garden. The old-fashioned man who dressed as though he was an eighteenth century gentleman. They were all different creatures, but for the first time, Laura realised that they were all the same - or at least, all of a type. The Dead Cat People. Suddenly they fused in the strange, electric atmosphere of the cat séance into an oddball gang. It was, Laura decided, a little like what would happen if you put two hundred cats in a room. They would not become an army, or a pack, but they would become something. All over the audience, conversations were breaking out. Numbers were being swapped. What could such a group do, if unleashed on the world, Laura wondered. Nothing probably. Probably...

One thing was certain, she would notice them from now on. She wouldn't overlook them now they had a name. Whenever she saw such un-placeable people in the street, she would know how to place them. They were the Dead Cat People.

Laura watched Ms. Blythe holding this group together with her strange, pantomime magic. She was like some kind of leader - a queen cat? Laura felt her metaphor starting to crumble. There were no queen cats.

Laura picked out another cat to bring to the audience. Then another. The Chuckle brothers went to a youngish man with pale, sunken cheeks who had lost his parents in quick succession the previous year. He had a beaten, haunted look which lifted instantly as he lifted the two cats.

Even Delia Smith was picked up instantly by a lady whose sister had electrocuted herself in the bath. If Laura knew Delia, it must have been an abusive relationship - and the woman had probably finally snapped and tossed the hair dryer into the bathwater herself. Laura wondered if getting the cat was a way to assuage her own guilt. Either way, one less for the hypodermic.

Laura decided not to bring out The Boston Strangler. The little kitten was only a few months old, and there was a tearful girl in the front row, searching the eyes of the cats as they came out. She was too damaged. Too desperate. Ms. Blythe might be willing to take advantage, but to Laura, there was a line, and sending The Boston Strangler home with a recently bereaved kid crossed it somehow.

"Don't you think this is dishonest?" Laura asked Judy, who was sitting in a corner counting the takings. Judy looked at her, puzzled.

"Why would you feel the need to ask that question?" She said.

"These people think they're their dead relatives." said Laura. "Surely that's wrong. In reality they're just cats."

"Reality?" said Judy, puzzled, "That may be your reality. It's not theirs. Who are we to force our reality on others?"

She counted another handful of ten pound notes into the cash box, "Everybody's reality is equally valid."

But, thought Laura, everybody's reality was not equally valid. Some people's reality was just wrong.

Ms. Blythe was just wrapping up the evening. Laura scanned the hopeful eyes of the audience. The place was buzzing. She brought up the house lights and people began to file slowly towards the door. Then, she saw him. Right at the back, standing silently, his face in shadow, it was the thick necked man. The cat murderer from the funeral!

The moment she spotted him, his eyes flicked up to the lighting desk where she was sitting. He knew she'd seen him. Instantly he started fighting his way to the front of the stage, pushing through the energised crowd of Dead Cat People, clambering over rows of seats.

Laura ducked backstage, thinking fast. If he was back, there could only be one reason. He was looking for Christof. They needed to run. Christof was in his box by the door, curled up next to the disfigured face of Princess Anne. She reached out to grab him. That was when she spotted Gordon Ramsey, pressed up against the side of his cage. He was about the same size as Christof and a similar grey colour. At a distance, you could confuse them. Laura grabbed the celebrity chef, tucked him under her arm and pelted for the stage door just as the cat killer threw open the curtain and burst through.

The stage door lead to the building's fire escape and Laura ran down the stairs and out into the dark alley behind the theatre. Gordon was struggling, and his claws were out, digging into the back of her hand, but she held on. Behind her, she heard the cat killer crash out of the fire escape, kicking over a dustbin. He cursed and ran after her.

Laura was not a fast runner. The only thing she practiced on the school sports field was her look of disdain. It was withering, but it wasn't going to help her much now. However, she did know the university campus pretty well. She had wandered it furiously on many evenings, while waiting for Peter to finish his unfinishable work. At the end of the alley, she made a sharp right between the old decaying building of the original college, and the new decaying building of the technology labs.

The cat killer skidded around the corner behind her, and crashed into the wall. He cursed, and then stumbled after her. Laura could hear him closing in.

"Stop!" he shouted. It was an accent she couldn't place. As if, thought Laura, "Stop, or I shoot!" Shoot? She looked round. He had pulled out a gun. An actual gun!

She dived into a turning to her left. People didn't have guns. Not in real life.

The rest of the campus would be empty at night. The Dead Cat People would be filing out through the theatre, but the only way back there was to loop around through the underground car park. It was a long run, and she was slowing already.

She could hear the man behind her. He was close. She thought fast. He'd be an idiot to fire while he was running. He'd be likely to miss, and he'd attract the attention of everyone on the campus. Of course, that was no guarantee that he wouldn't. His credentials as an idiot were already well proven, given the fact he was trying to carry out a contract killing on a cat.

Up ahead, the narrow alley between the two buildings ended abruptly. If she ran straight across the courtyard, he'd be able to stop and take his shot. Instead, she ducked to the side, and sprinted, carrying the struggling cat, along the side of the building.

Behind her, she heard a soft, "Phut," sound, and to her left, a pane of glass exploded. So much for her pursuer waiting for a clear shot. He had a silencer. Who had silencers, she wondered. She answered the question in her head instantly: People with guns - they had silencers. People with guns which they used to shoot people had silencers. That was who had silencers!

Laura started screaming. Panicked wordless yelling in between gasping for air as she raced towards the edge of the building and the next alleyway. She figured any sound that might bring help would unnerve her attacker, but it didn't seem to be working. As she reached the corner, he was almost at her back again.

She slowed a fraction, dodged right, and then swerved suddenly into the alleyway. Behind her, she heard the man grunt in his un-placable accent. He had fallen for her dummy and missed the turning.

She had a couple of seconds while he skidded to a halt and turned back. In front of her, there was a fire door into one of the buildings. She aimed a kick at the bar shaped handle, but as it flew open, she pushed herself back flat against the opposite wall crouching behind a rubbish bin.

A second later, she heard the man pounding down the alley towards her. He could see that the path in front of him was empty, and that the fire door was swinging on its hinges. Laura watched him dive through the doors and scramble up the stairs, then she ran down the alley and threw herself down the concrete spiral stairs into the car park.

At the bottom, she stopped, breathing hard. She slumped against the wall, trying to calm the struggling cat.

The back of her hand was red with scratches, and blood was beginning to seep out of them, smearing over her hands.

The light from the staircase spilled out into the underground car park, mixing with the cool, flickering strip lights which made little pools of light around the few remaining cars. The place was empty except for the flapping of pigeons roosting in the ceiling.

Suddenly, there was a sound above her. Footsteps on the stairs, stumbling down. The shadow of a gun on the wall.

Laura ran. If she could make it across to the exit, she would be out in front of the theatre. The slowest of the old ladies in the crowd would still be chattering their way across to the train station. If her pursuer wanted to avoid witnesses there, he would have to instigate a massacre. Either that, or rely on his lawyer's ability to discredit the testimony of a bunch of octogenarians visiting a cat séance...

It was her only chance. There was the "Phut" sound again, and a spark as a bullet ricocheted off a car next to her. She dodged, and ran on. The door was right in front of her. She threw herself at it hard, barging with her shoulder.

There was a jarring pain, but the door didn't move. Her heart sank. It was locked. Of course it was locked. Everyone had gone home. She'd lost count of the number of times she had rushed Peter from his work to get to the car park before it closed. It was a stupid mistake. She felt a little embarrassed.

She spun around. No escape now. Her embarrassment was unlikely to last long. The man was walking calmly towards her, raising the gun.

She did the only thing she could do. She threw Gordon Ramsey at him. Later, she would wonder whether throwing a cat at a man with a gun was the wisest move she could have made. Later, she would ask herself just what she thought the action might have achieved. What, she would wonder, was the goal which flashed through her mind at the time? Did she think he would drop the gun, and stagger backwards as the animal clamped over his face, digging its claws deep into the soft fleshy parts of his jowls? Did she imagine he would turn and flee at the sight of an airborne blue-Persian cross-breed? If the plan had gone well, what would it have achieved?

But the plan, whatever it was, did not go well.

The cat arced through the air, spinning to land claws first, but the thick-necked man simply raised his hand. The gun jolted and Gordon Ramsey hit the floor, quite dead.

Laura stared.

Slowly, the man raised his gun again, this time he was aiming at her. She put her hands in the air - it felt a little silly, but she was pretty sure it was what you were supposed to do in such circumstances. She saw him squeeze the trigger.

Suddenly, he was hit from the side, by another figure, flying out of the darkness. The gun jolted and a fluorescent bulb above her head exploded. She heard a grunt and a fleshy thud as the two men hit the floor together, and the gun spun off, clattering under a car.

The scuffle only lasted a few seconds. The initial surprise of the attack had caught the cat killer off balance, but the new man was a hopeless fighter. His arms flailed and gangled. His slight body was no match for the stocky assassin. A single punch left the new man clutching his face, and a powerful kick sent him crashing against a car. The alarm shrieked into life as the man swayed and shook his head.

The cat killer stepped back, raising his fist, but as he heard the sound of the alarm, he froze. Clearly he didn't want to risk being discovered. He looked from the new man to Laura and back, then down to the dead body of Gordon Ramsey on the floor. Then he turned and ran back across the car park, up the stairs and out of sight.

"Are you OK?" Laura asked the other man. He was leaning against the car, his thin body hunched over, head in hands.

The man made a noise that could have signified almost anything. Laura approached. There was something familiar about the bony, slightly awkward figure.

"Dr. Dan?" She said. "What are you doing here?" The celebrity doctor stood up, and dropped his hands away from his face. A cut on his lip was starting to swell, and his eye looked red. Next time he was on a comedy panel show, he'd be in make-up for a long time.

He grinned his trademark grin, a little lopsided now.

"Oh, just passing," he said.

"Don't give me that crap, someone just tried to kill me!" Laura shouted, "Gordon Ramsey is dead," she added. Dr. Dan looked at the dead cat.

"You mean this isn't Christof?" he asked with obvious relief.

"No."

He looked puzzled. "Why not?"

Why indeed? When Laura had grabbed Gordon Ramsey instead of Christof, she had done it on instinct. She had done it to protect Christof, but she had not thought about it. But why? Christof was just a cat, like any other cat. And Laura didn't even like cats. She told herself it had just been because of Grandad's puzzle. Because Christof was part of some bigger mystery, but the truth was simpler than that. The truth was that she was beginning to like the irritating creature.

"This was the cat I was holding," she lied. "He must have thought it was Christof," Laura looked at the floor. Poking out under the bonnet of the car was the attacker's gun. She stooped to pick it up. It felt heavy and dangerous in her hand. "Are you going to explain to me what you were doing here?"

"I heard about your cat séance. I was intrigued."

"So you followed me into the car park?"

"I saw him in the audience. I followed him," he said.

"Maybe I'll just take you to the police," she said.

"With what? With a dead cat, and a gun with your fingerprints on it?" Laura looked down at the gun, her hand wrapped around the handle. Her finger naturally curling round the trigger. "Do you think you could point it in a different direction?" Dr. Dan added, nervously.

"Tell me what's going on!" she almost yelled at him.

Dr. Dan looked suddenly serious, "I'm sorry," he said, "I'm bound." Laura looked puzzled.

"Bound? What does that mean?"

"Bound by the terms of your grandfather's will," he said, "I can't tell you, until you work it out for yourself. He was quite specific." Laura stared at him. "Find out who Christof is."

"I already have," she said, "It doesn't help."

"Look again," said Dr. Dan.

The celebrity scientist brushed himself down, picked up the dead cat by the tail, and walked off into the darkness.

"What if he comes back?" she shouted after him.

"You've got a gun," Dr. Dan shouted back.

When Laura got back, Peter and Judy did not ask where she had been. They did not wonder why she was so flushed when she returned, and they did not ask why her bag was bulging with a hard, metal shape. Parents.

They did notice Gordon was missing, but put it down to an administrative error - cats had been flying thick and fast that evening, and both Laura's parents assumed he'd been palmed off on some unsuspecting victim while they were busy counting the money. Gordon Ramsey, it was unanimously agreed by the family, had gone to a better place.

The couple were on a high. They had raised more cash than they could have hoped, and shrunk the Dead Cat Quota as well. Peter started off by babbling about making the event a monthly one, but within minutes he was talking about syndicating pet séances nationwide, and starting a course to teach animal mediums at the university. The Principal, he felt sure, would jump at the chance. After all, it would bring in lucrative students from the States and Asia, at a time when the University was struggling...

Ms. Blythe listened carefully, but said nothing.

Chapter 8: Christof Arises

One of Laura's firm rules was that Christof was absolutely never allowed to enter her bedroom, but the night of the séance, she decided to make an exception. In fact, it was less of an exception, and more of a final acceptance that her rule was over.

Christof lay, curled up at the end of her bed. She needed him there, warm and soft, because the other thing on her bed was not warm and soft. It was cold and hard. A loaded gun with a silencer, and her fingerprints all over it. A murder weapon which she had seen in action, but had no idea how to use, or where it came from. She didn't know how to disarm it, or whether the safety catch was on - or indeed if there was any such thing as a safety catch outside of gangster movies. The gun felt like a very dangerous thing to have around - especially when she knew there was a pretty good chance that her parents' present course of action would end with courtrooms and policemen and quite possibly bailiffs.

It was early morning by the time Laura finally gave up any attempt to sleep, and decided to do some serious thinking. Grandad was enacting some kind of plan from beyond the grave. It involved her, her cat, and, apparently, Dr. Dan Pan, the celebrity scientist, but she wasn't allowed to know what the plan was. There was a cat killer on the loose who had a gun that looked like it came from a spy movie. And somewhere in the mix of all this was the reclusive Christof Tourenski -

who shared at least one of his many diplomas with her surprisingly successful granny.

There was also the small matter of the impending court case against her parents, which the cat séance was not going to be enough to stop, the death of (now not quite) one hundred cats, and Granny (Sylvia) Gryene's offer to put her on the fast track to taking over her business.

Judy had warned Laura, in one of her excruciatingly one-sided parental counseling sessions, that teenage years were often complex and confusing. This kind of stuff probably happened to everyone, she thought.

Laura decided her first step had to be to get something to eat. She crept through the chaotic library of the hallway into the chaotic library of the kitchen and made herself a sandwich with the only ingredients that looked edible: honey roasted corn flakes. It was unconventional, but not unpleasant.

She laid it on her bed next to the cat and the gun, and she flipped open her tablet.

"Christof Tourenski" she typed. She expected the same thin trickle of results as before. What she saw made her sit straight up.

There were dozens of entries. Suddenly, Christof was all over the Internet.

An article in the Observer lifestyle section had appeared just after Laura had done her first search. It wasn't a news item, but more a life-affirming aspirational feature about the man's life. It was about time he got some recognition, thought Laura. The writer, a Josephine Gilliam, had done a pretty good job with limited material. The article appeared to be a reworking of the Wikipedia entry Laura had already seen. It contained nothing new, but included colourful descriptions, and stock photos of the exotic places Christof had visited in his strange, nomadic life. The journalist responsible had embellished on the Wiki page, but it was pretty clear that she had not spoken to Christof, or interviewed anyone who actually knew him.

However, the Observer appeared to be an influential publication, because following that, there was an article in the London Metro which suggested Christof might be hanging out in the capital's trendy districts around Whitechapel. Frustratingly for Laura, the piece didn't actually provide any concrete sightings in London, and its quotes seemed pretty vague. The entire article appeared to have been put together using a combination of the Observer piece, and the original Wikipedia article.

Laura read on down the list of search results. Several more articles had been penned by different journalists, in different blogs, newspapers and magazines, each being concocted by recombining the information in those published before it. Every one added a little detail to the story, either in the form of a piece of information about one of the places Christof had visited, or in the form of a quote from someone who hadn't actually met Christof, but who had a different perspective on some aspect of his life's work.

None of the journalists had managed to find Christof himself. He seemed to be sensibly keeping out of the limelight, so there was a battle going on to source quotes. The most fertile source of these was from practitioners in the various alternative therapies he had become an expert in. Anxious to promote their own work and ideas, they were delighted to add their own reputations to Christof's. Gushing quotes about how well Christof's work enhanced the benefits of their own helped build both their reputations, and Christof's. It was an ever expanding media love-bomb.

The most recent features about Christof had started to include quotes from someone they described as an "expert" in matters relating to Christof Tourenski's life. Laura quickly scanned the article. Maybe this expert could help her. Eventually, she found a name. The expert was none other than Josephine Gilliam - the writer of the original piece published just a few days previously in the Observer.

Christof's life seemed to appeal the interests of readers of a huge range of different publications. Health magazines focused on his treatments. Travel magazines mentioned him when they covered the places he had visited. Political commentators dropped his name into blogs on foreign policy and food bloggers championing the medicinal benefits of herbs and miracle foods used his work to bolster the credentials of their recipes.

Within a week, Christof Tourenski had gone from a little known recluse to a media sensation. His life had been pretty wide ranging, so early articles had struggled to give him a pithy title. However, before long, one phrase started to crop up over and over: "Alternative Health Guru" Christof Tourneski Mhp, PD, T, MNBA, FHsoc, AS became the more easily digested, "Alternative Health Guru, Christof Tourenski" and before long, everyone who mentioned him, used the same title. It seemed to fit, and it made it perfectly clear who Christof was, and what he was about.

But there remained one question. In all this, where was Christof? None of the articles she read pointed to where he might be, or what he might have to do with Grandad.

She was just about to scroll on to the next search page, when she was suddenly, and violently sick. It was instant. She didn't feel sick, she just was sick. She looked down. Lumps of cornflake sandwich and bile covered the gun. She looked to her side. The remains of the sandwich sat next to her. For the first time, she noticed that the corner of the crust was thick with green and white mold. She felt the feeling rising in her stomach, and vomited again almost immediately.

Christof Tourenski left the bed.

Now, she felt it. Wave after wave of nausea sweeping over her, clogging her throat, her nose, her brain. She clambered, dizzy from the bed. She had to make it to the toilet. She staggered towards the door, holding her mouth.

No.

The first thing she had to do was hide the gun. The illegal, loaded, dangerous, sick covered gun. She forced her hand to reach out and grab it. It was slippery and cold. She picked it up and shoved it under the bed. Then she vomited again. This time on the floor.

Chapter 9: Guns and Pills and Social Media

"And what else?" Laura had already been answering the man's questions for about three quarters of an hour, and he showed no signs of running out.

"Nothing else," she said through gritted teeth, "I ate some bread with mold on it, and then I was sick. I just need some medicine to stop me from being sick."

There was, said Judy, no point in trying to get an appointment with a regular doctor. Admin changes at the local surgery meant that you couldn't book an appointment more than or less than 48 hours in advance. You had to know when you were going to be ill, and book your six minute appointment exactly two days ahead. It was, Judy said, a way to reduce waiting lists.

Instead, she had bundled Laura into the car and rushed her to the consulting room of her favourite homeopath. Dr. Halls had prescribed the pills which were the only cure for Judy's headaches, and she would, Judy assured Laura, make short work of a bit of food poisoning.

Short work, however, had turned out to be something Dr. Halls, or Barry, as he insisted on being called, prided himself on not doing. His surgery was light and airy, and contained many pot plants. Laura had decided she didn't like him within about thirty seconds, but she extended him the courtesy of not throwing up on him and tried to answer his questions.

They were wide-ranging and exhaustive. He asked about her aches and pains. He asked about her hopes for the future. He asked about the things that made her stressed. In answering this, she didn't give him the full list - that would have taken weeks. She didn't mention her stupid parents, or men with guns, or TV personalities, or feline reincarnation. Instead she made up some teenage stuff she thought he might like. She vaguely mentioned exams, and how she couldn't believe The Ice Crystals were splitting up. Barry seemed fascinated.

He asked a lot about her diet. She didn't feel it was fair to her parents to be entirely truthful about the contents and hygiene levels of their kitchen. She also didn't think she could accurately describe either without vomiting again. Instead she gave a gave a version which was sanitised - in both senses of the word.

After every answer, Barry gave a thoughtful expression, and typed something into his computer. He then turned back to her, paused, and said the words "...And what else?"

She felt as though he was caring for her, that he was taking time to look after her whole being. That he was really trying to thoroughly understand her problem. However, her problem was that she was feeling sick, and she needed pills that would stop her feeling sick. It wasn't, she wanted to scream at his gentle, caring face, brain surgery.

Time and again, she tried to steer the conversation back to the matter of her upset stomach, and time and again, he would divert to the subject of her whole being. It was like trying to hold two repelling magnets together,

Eventually he got around to asking about the sandwich.

"What was in it?" he said.

"Moldy bread," said Laura.

"Bread isn't good. Was it processed?" he said, "was it white bread?"

"It was green!"

"Gluten is a real problem," he said, "Butter?"

"No butter." she said.

"Unlikely to be a lactose issue, then."

"I think," said Laura, trying one last time, and hoping he didn't ask about the cornflakes, "that it may have been a problem with mold."

Finally, Laura and Judy left with a small bottle of yellow pills labeled Arsenicum 30c, and instructions to dissolve them under her tongue. She took one in the car, and resigned herself to feeling sick for the rest of the week.

Then she saw the logo on the packaging. "Gryene's" it said in large, friendly letters. These pills were made at the impressive factory of Sylvia Gryene. They may work after all, she thought.

By the time she got home, she was feeling a lot better. Sylvia Gryene's pills were clearly powerful stuff. The waves of nausea were reducing all the time, and her stomach felt less like it had been hit by a crowbar.

She was, however, very tired. She slept solidly for the rest of the day, and fitfully through the night. Through the early hours, images repeated themselves in her head. Gordon Ramsey flying through the air. The soft sound of the gunshot. The body thudding lifeless into the concrete floor. Over and over. Each time she tried to pick him up. To cradle him.

If she could only picture that in her mind, there might be some kind of end to the loop. But she could not picture it because it had not happened. She had not cradled the little body, or comforted him. She had never done that in his entire caged life. She had used him. Chosen him as less valuable than Christof. Dragged him from his cage. Thrown him at her attacker, and watched him take the bullet. Then she had left him there - not even glanced at the corpse. She had been too busy. Not even bothered to remove the body. She had watched Dr. Dan pick him up by the tail and walk away. Collateral damage. And now she was paying for it with her dreams. Cats.

And every time she broke free of the images, and struggled to reality, there was the gun under her bed. She could feel it. She could smell it. The sticky iron smell of metal and sick. She had taken the gun, and left the cat. That, she thought, was Laura all over.

And there were ninety more where he came from. Dead Cat Day must not happen.

When it came, she was glad of the sound of letters through the door. It meant that it was morning. The night was over. She forced herself out of bed, wrapped a dressing gown around her, and struggled downstairs. The contents of the kitchen were no better and no more appetising than they had been before. Judy and Peter were in an ongoing standoff over who was going to do the shopping, and Laura knew this would continue until one of them could stand the squalor no longer. Normally, that person was Laura, but today she was in no condition to shop for groceries. They would have to sort it out for themselves.

On the doormat was the morning paper - the headline read "Government inquiry into alternative medicine - experts to give evidence." She ignored it, grabbed the mail from the doormat and climbed back into bed.

Her head was pounding, and she reached for another of Granny Gryene's pills. Maybe, if they did their work, she could be up and around by tomorrow. As she let it dissolve under her tongue, she looked at the bottle again. Stuck to the back of the packaging was Dr. Halls' card. After his name, the qualification, Master of Homeopathic Prescription was printed after his name. Mhp? Laura jumped. Another one of Christof's qualifications. The one in Granny Gryene's office had been about the production of homeopathic cures. This one was in prescribing them. Granny Gryene understood the production of her medicine, but not its prescription. Dr. Halls had apparently mastered its usage. Christof Tourenski had studied both. It made sense. She tapped Google on her tablet. Another complex and structured course. Another range of self-study options. Another indignant dismissal from the pompous Melvin Rochester. Laura was beginning to think that anything that annoyed Melvin Rochester must be worth a second look.

She closed the tablet, and turned her attention to the bundle of letters. It was surprisingly large.

The top one was addressed in hastily scrawled writing to Christof Tourenski. She flicked through the rest. They were all addressed to Christof Tourenski. Every letter. She tore open the top one. It was from Josephine Gilliam, the Observer journalist. She was looking for an interview. Of course she was! With her growing reputation as an expert in all things Christof, she was being constantly asked to deliver quotes for other articles. Since all she had to reference was the contents of the original Wiki page, her well of expertise was going to run dry pretty quickly. Apparently, she fronted a talk-show on daytime TV - which Laura had never seen - and wanted to invite Christof to appear.

The letter sounded, to be honest, a little desperate. She even suggested that if Christof wanted to maintain his silence, he could send a representative of his choice. Josephine clearly saw a rich seam of future journalistic work opening up for her if she could become the sole spokesperson for Christof Tourenski, and she wasn't going to quit until she found him. Laura felt almost like writing back, but she didn't think "meaow" was going to cut it.

She opened the next. It was from a radio DJ looking for an on air interview. Then there were a couple more journalists seeking interviews, and she skimmed through them with a growing sense of worry.

It was only a matter of time before one of these tenacious journalists decided to simply pop round for a chat. For all she knew, they could be hiding in the garden right now. If they were, she pitied them. Not only were they on a goose chase so wild that they were chasing the wrong species, but the garden was mostly nettles and brambles.

She looked at the envelopes again. None of them had her address. All the letters were addressed, not to her postcode, but to a PO box. Laura knew about PO boxes from Grandad. They were a simple forwarding system which you could register instead of an address. Whenever anyone sent something to the PO box, it would be delivered to the address you gave them without the sender ever having to know where you were. Businesses used them all the time, and so did anyone else who either moved around a lot, or just wanted to keep their whereabouts private.

So why did Chirstof have one, how did the journalists know what it was, and why did it point to her address?

Laura flipped open her tablet and found Christof's Wiki page. Sure enough, in a footnote, the PO box number was listed. That was it, then; anyone could edit a Wiki page, so that narrowed the culprit down to - anyone. But Christof the cat's real address was only known to a few people. This was

Grandad. Laura had no doubt. He had set up a PO box and added the footnote to the Wiki page before he died so that Laura got all the real Christof Tourenski's mail.

But why?

On a whim, she searched his name again. This time there were even more search entries.

It seemed that Christof's period of silence was over. He was now speaking to the world through the medium of internet memes. A series of quotes was popping up on Facebook and Twitter, being shared and re-shared, liked and posted with gathering speed.

"The greatest medicine of all is to teach people not to need it," said one.

Another read: "Let your food be your medicine and your medicine be your food". Each one was printed in a friendly font and overlaid onto images of oceans, or forests, and under each quote, the same accreditation: "Christof Tourenski Mhp, PD, T, MNBA, FHsoc, AS"

Pretty good stuff, thought Laura. Christof was turning out to be every bit as interesting as his Wiki page had suggested. She was starting to believe that part of Grandad's plan was for Christof to become her personal guide.

Another quote bobbed onto the screen: "We cannot solve our problems with the same thinking we used when we created them." This one had a familiar ring to it. Had she heard it before? If it was taken from some work by Christof, she might be able to find that. She typed it in quotation marks into Google and hit return.

Multiple references appeared immediately. The quote wasn't by Christof. It was credited to

Albert Einstein. Fair enough, thought Laura. That kind of thing happened fairly often. Quotes got adapted and adopted. She searched another of Christof's quotes. It turned out to be by Hippocrates. In fact, every one of the carefully inscribed Christof memes turned out to be somebody else's quote. Another dead end. Still, thought Laura, at least the memes were bringing Christof to a wider audience. That had to be good, didn't it?

But there was a more pressing concern. The gun. The gun was a clue. It must be. Murder investigations always made a big thing out of finding the murder weapon, so it must be important. The gun, of course, wasn't Grandad's murder weapon. He hadn't been shot, but no detective story she'd ever read gave advice about murders where cancer was the weapon of choice. She had the gun, and it was clearly important to find out as much as she could about it, and then offload it as quickly as possible.

And there was one person she knew who would be able to help with both of those things.

Samuel was not exactly a friend. He was a classmate, and he liked her. Liked her in a sort of creepy, too-scared-to-talk-to-her kind of way. More importantly, he knew about guns. He could tell you the make and model of guns used in every movie and every videogame you didn't want to hear about. He could describe their effects in great detail, and given the chance, he would.

On reflection, the fact that Samuel was too scared to talk to her most of the time was probably the best thing about Samuel.

Samuel had a holiday job in a military memorabilia shop - a strange, dark little shop with Wild West flags and World War I helmets hanging outside. It was the sort of place Laura never went to. In fact, it was pretty obvious nobody else ever went there either. As she walked in, Samuel looked up from his magazine as though she'd just walked into his living room.

She opened her bag, pulled out the gun, and put it on the counter.

"What can you tell me about this?" she said.

"It's got cornflakes on it," said Samuel.

"Yes," she said, "anything else?"

"It's a replica of course," he said, trying to show off, "and not a very good one." He picked the gun up, and seemed surprised by its weight. Before she could say anything, he waved it playfully in the air, holding it sideways in the style of a gangster movie, and squeezed the trigger.

The recoil threw his hand back so that he hit himself hard in the stomach, and collapsed. A display case shattered on the other side of the shop. Samuel dropped the gun.

"It's a real gun," said Laura, unnecessarily.

"It's - it's a real gun!" repeated Samuel incredulously, struggling to his feet.

"I was hoping you could tell me about it," she said.

"It's a real gun."

"I was hoping for something more specific than that," she smiled in a way that she hoped would suggest that this was his big chance to impress her. He stepped forward, gingerly, and looked down at the gun. He was visibly shaking.

Gathering himself, he gently stroked the barrel as though it was an animal. "It's a Truvelo Advanced Defensive Pistol" he said. "It was designed in the early 90's to be easily hidden in your clothing."

"Ok," said Laura. "What I really want to know is who would have one?"

"It's not rare. But I'm surprised it's turned up here."

"Why?"

"It's made in Africa for private security companies - that sort of thing." He paused, "Where did you get it?"

"I found it in a car park," she said. "I need to get rid of it." His eyes lit up instantly.

"I could take it. Can I take it?" He said eagerly. He was grinning broadly - his breath coming in little gasps of excitement.

Samuel taking the gun off her hands was exactly what she had hoped for, but now that she was here, it didn't seem quite such a great plan. Samuel would take the gun. He'd be delighted to. And he would know the right thing to do with it.

But Samuel would not do the right thing. Samuel was gun-obsessed, and a bit too keen on violent video games, and a bit too keen on Laura. He was harmless enough, but once he had a gun, he would not be harmless anymore.

Suddenly, as she looked into his excited eyes, she could see a future where he realised that the accountancy course his parents had forced him into taking was going to lead him into decades of drudgery. Where his soul would be slowly burned away, leaving only suppressed rage. Samuel was just the kind of quiet, slightly shy, conscientious chap who eventually went on a killing spree.

Laura could quite foresee a time when he would be holding her hostage in an upstairs room, while taking potshots at surrounding policemen out of the window.

She smiled, and put the gun back into her bag. It would have to go back under her bed for now. Samuel did not need a gun. Samuel needed a kitten.

The next morning, Laura felt a lot better, but the postman brought a whole new bundle of letters. Christof Tourenski's reach was growing. Alongside the journalists' requests, another kind of letter had started to emerge.

The first was from a gentleman named Bernard. Bernard had what he described as wonky knees. He had always had wonky knees and it had just been a part of his life. However, over the last couple of years, things had been getting worse for Bernard. His knees had started to give him pain, so doctors prescribed rest, then when that didn't work, they offered painkillers.

Matters only got worse. They x-rayed and found nothing wrong. They checked him for arthritis, for damage to the ligaments, and even for gout, and they found nothing. And all the time, the pain was increasing. Nothing helped, and once the doctors found nothing wrong, they discharged him. Bernard could, by now, barely walk. With no diagnosis, he was passed as fit to work, but he couldn't work. He could hardly leave his home. Fired from his job, and with no help and no treatment, he could take no exercise and he started to gain weight. This made it even harder for him to walk, and the cycle continued.

At the time of writing, Bernard, a once happy and active man, was alone, isolated, and falling into depression. He was prepared, he said, to try anything that Christof could recommend. Any cure, however outlandish or unproven. Bernard was at the end of the line.

The second letter was from a woman whose daughter had been hit by a drunk driver. She enclosed a photo of the six-year-old child, and described her daily trips to the intensive care unit where the only indication that her daughter still lived was the slow beep of the heart monitor, and the changing numbers on the computer screen next to her.

The letter was an act of desperation. This mother catalogued in detail every injury to her daughter's body, external and internal, and every treatment that had failed to revive her. Laura read about the crushing pain of standing day after day, week after week at the bedside of an unresponsive child. The fear at every moment she was with her, and the guilt of every moment she could not be. Waiting and worrying at every alarm that went off at the hospital, and every phone that rang when she was away. The letter ended with a plea to Christof - a prayer almost - that he had to help because, as the mother repeated, constantly throughout her letter, almost as the only straw she had to cling to: everything happened for a reason.

She opened a few more. They were desperate, pitiful and often heartrending. From people who had been told medical science could do nothing for them, to those with minor ailments which had become so debilitating that sufferers had nowhere else to turn. From problems which doctors failed to explain to diseases which medical science could diagnose, but could do nothing to cure. Christof's story was acting like a beacon of hope to anyone in pain. They wrote to him asking for help, advice, guidance of any and every kind. Laura was moved. These people were desperate. They had been failed, they told her, over and over again. The doctors had no answers for them. Time and again, they were sent away with pills they knew would not work - or with nothing but vague advice that they should eat better, or rest - or worse, with the conclusion that there was simply nothing wrong with them.

Laura sat on her bed, surrounded by the letters. She didn't know when this became her problem, but somehow it had. These people needed help, and helping them was now her job - as if she needed another one. If she could somehow find the real Christof Tourenski, then perhaps she could pass the letters on. But how?

She picked up another letter at random and it made her stop abruptly. It was addressed to Christof, but the address was not the PO box. This was the correct address. Her address. She tore open the envelope.

She realised she must be getting paranoid. It was just a note from the vet. A checkup she'd scheduled weeks ago for Christof.

Her phone rang. From the other room, she could hear Judy shouting, "I wonder whether the shopping has been done? Laura?"

"I'm sick, remember?" Laura shouted back.

"Hello? I'm calling about Christof Tourenski. Did you get my letter?" said the voice at the other end. It must be the vet, thought Laura.

"Hi, yes," she glanced down at the date of the appointment." Damn, it was today. "Is it about today?" she said trying to sound as though it had been in her diary all along.

"That's right," the voice wasn't a receptionist she knew. "Are you sure you're OK with it?"

"Why wouldn't I be?" said Laura brightly.

"And you're going to be speaking on his behalf?"

"Well, he won't be speaking for himself," she said.

"No, I suppose not. I'll send a car now." The line went dead. A car? Since when did the vet send a car for you? Grandad must have taken out quite some insurance policy.

It wasn't until she was actually in the car with Christof, that it occurred to her that that the call probably hadn't been from the vet. As they pulled up outside the big building and were met at the door by a smiling woman who never stopped talking, Laura decided that she would learn most if she just kept her mouth shut and said "yes" to anything she was asked.

It was a policy which would have worked well had she not been taking part in an interview on live TV.

Laura was bundled from one waiting room to the next by the talkative (but deeply uninformative) PA, until without warning, she found herself on an orange sofa, surrounded by cameras in front of an astoundingly over made-up bright orange host whose hair smelt as though she used battery acid as hairspray.

"Hello, I'm Josephine Gilliam," she said.

Nobody asked Laura why she had a cat on a lead with her, and she didn't volunteer any information on the subject. They probably assumed that if the mysterious guru, Christof Tourenski was going to use a teenage girl as some kind of mouthpiece, then he might well be eccentric enough to present her carrying a cat.

Laura did learn that this particular show had, in previous weeks, played host to an artist who ate only flowers; a woman who believed she was Jesus; a football player who thought the royal family were aliens; and a pop star who had been known to wear dresses made from raw meat. Laura and her pet cat must have represented a fairly standard day at the office.

The cartoonish Gilliam introduced Laura to the viewers as the mouthpiece of the elusive and fascinating Christof Tourenski, whose experiences and ideas were changing the way the world looked at alternative medicine. Gilliam turned to her and seemed to be expecting her to say something wise and important.

"Yes," said Laura.

There was a long silence.

"He must be fascinating to work with," she said.

"Yes," said Laura. There was another long silence.

Josephine Gilliam was beginning to flounder. "And Christof claims to work with herbal cures, and treatments designed by witch doctors, and traditional Indian and Chinese medicine?"

"Yes," said Laura.

Gilliam whirled round. Her hair stayed with her as though it was set in concrete. "I'd like you to welcome my other guest, Professor Melvin Rochester."

Great, thought Laura. The world's most obnoxious man. She wondered whether he remembered her shouting at him for upsetting Granny Gryene at Grandad's funeral. As he was ushered into the seat opposite her, his eyebrows were giving nothing away.

"And what do you think of all this?" said the host.

"It's all a load of utter, utter nonsense," he said, "there is not the tiniest shred of empirical evidence for anything this charlatan claims."

"So you don't believe any alternative medicine can possibly work?"

"Some of it - yes. But when alternative medicine is shown to work, it's not alternative anymore. It's just medicine. There may be treatments that have an effect on isolated individuals but how would we know whether these are due to chance unless it had been properly tested? It's all just a load of nonsense!"

Gilliam turned back to Laura. She said nothing, but pulled a face like an expectant duck which she held, staring straight at Laura until it became clear that the answer "yes" just wasn't going to do this time.

Laura paused. She had seen enough professors in her time to see this arrogant act for what it was. Peter and his friends had tried it on her ever since she could remember, and she was immune. It was time to put this self-righteous bully in his place.

"This morning," she started, "I got a letter from a man named Bernard..."

The moment she started telling Bernard's story, it was as if something took over inside her. Anger - outrage that these people were being let down by conventional medicine, and that this scientist, this arrogant, heartless man would take the one shred of hope they had left and dismiss it as though it was nothing. No, she thought. This would not stand.

Suddenly she was fluent. She was not just going to sit meekly and say 'yes' to everything! This was important. This needed to be said. She brought up letter after letter. Case after case from Christof's bulging postbag. The man whose crippling hay fever kept him housebound for six months of the year. The woman whose child had been diagnosed with autism just weeks after she was assured that the vaccinations he had been given could do no harm. Case after case - each one, she jabbed her finger at Rochester as she told him, was not a statistic. Not a point on a graph, but a real person with real feelings.

The sight of this girl in black, and her shabby cat tearing into the respected scientist must have been quite something. Certainly, Josephine Gilliam was beaming when she finally cut in to tell them their time was up, and that she had to move on to a feature about the decision of teen sensation, The Ice Crystals to put aside their artistic differences and perform one last gig.

"Well done! I didn't think you'd be so good" said Rochester, as they sat in the green room after the show waiting for their cars home.

"What?" stormed Laura.

"You did very well," he said. "I was beginning to think you were serious!"

"I was serious!" What an odious man, thought Laura.

"When did you work it out?" he said.

"Work what out?" Suddenly, her mind was spinning. "Did you set all this up? Did you give them my number?" Rochester stared back. "How did you even have my number?" she demanded.

Melvin Rochester glared at her, genuinely surprised. "Haven't you looked in the box?" he snapped.

"What box?"

"The papers that your grandfather gave you with the cat."

Laura stared at him. "There were no papers," she said. "Just a few vet's documents." She vaguely remembered Grandad handing her a box of papers. She'd glanced at the top ones at the time. They were vaccination forms, insurance details, vet's bills - all the usual bumpf. She'd given them to Judy who had doubtless shoved them into what passed for a filing system in the cat's home office.

"Look at them," said Rochester. He stared at her from under his eyebrows as though she was an idiot, "Go home and look at them right now, and then decide which side you're on."

Chapter 10: The Real Christof Tourenski

Searching the filing system in the tiny office of Kennington Paws worked pretty much in the same way as panning for gold. You picked your spot on the desk, or in one of the mysterious filing cabinets, you grabbed an arm full of papers and you sifted through them rejecting the stuff you didn't want until, if you were very lucky, you would what you were looking for, or at least one tantalizing piece of it.

Today, Laura found the process doubly difficult because two other things were going on in the office at the same time. Firstly, Peter was directing workers who had been hired with the money from the séance, to repair, repaint and update the most squalid parts of the home in an attempt to convince the authorities that the home was not on its last legs. And secondly, Judy was reading, and re-reading a court summons in an attempt to find a positive way of interpreting the fact that all the work was now for nothing. The NLFPC were not going to back off, and the case was going to court. If the hearing went against them, which it certainly would, then nothing but a miracle would be able to stop Dead Cat Day.

On the plus side, their work had meant that both her parents had been far too busy to be watching daytime TV, so her live appearance could, she hoped be quietly ignored.

In the meantime, she needed to find Christof's papers. Her first search was under C for Christof and T for Tourenski in the cat adoptions filing cabinet. She knew that this was a long shot, but thought the papers might turn up there as part of some elaborate double bluff. They didn't.

Nor were they anywhere in that filing cabinet, or the "miscellaneous" cabinet into which everything from cat litter receipts to actual cat litter was randomly stuffed. She looked behind the cabinets, on and under the desk and in the bookshelf. No luck.

Eventually, she decided to check the window sill. The only objects stored there were about a dozen boxes of liquor chocolates. Liquor chocolates tended to pile up in the office as the traditional gift old ladies would use to show their gratitude at the home either taking a cat from them, or giving one to them. Neither Judy nor Peter could stand the things, so they sat on the window sill slowly decaying.

She picked them up and dumped them in the waste bin. As she did so, she noticed the bottom box wasn't a chocolate box. It was a box file with the words "documents: Christof Tourenski" scrawled on it in Grandad's handwriting.

Laura grabbed it, left the chaos of the office, and hurried home.

She carefully laid the file on her bed. Christof himself hopped up to have a look, and she brushed him out of the way. The cat idly circled the box, and sat at the end of the bed, looking on.

Laura opened the box. Whatever Melvin Rochester had meant, the contents of the box were just as she expected. She flicked through them. Vet's certificates. Insurance. Inoculations. Nothing out of the ordinary. She picked the papers out of the box. The wad was a bit thicker than it should have been.

She flicked to the back. The last six papers were thicker than normal copy paper. Higher quality. She pulled them out, and stared at the top one.

It was a certificate. Printed on heavy embossed paper, decorative swirls surrounded the page in an ornate border like a picture frame. In the centre, a swirling signature, and next to that, a gold circle with a coat of arms embossed into it, and a red ribbon beneath. Above the signature, the words, "This is to certify that Christof Tourenski has satisfied the requirements of the examiners, and is therefore awarded, with Honours, the Diploma in Natural Alternative Therapies

She looked at the next page. It was Christof's award as a Master of Homeopathic Prescription. She flicked through. They were all here. All of Christof's awards in all their official glory ready to be framed and displayed on the walls of his surgery, or qualify him for access to committees, conferences and debates on live TV.

Laura stared at the pages, and then up at the cat watching her from the end of the bed. These were not copies, they were original documents.

And that could mean only one thing; her cat was not named after Christof Tourenski Mhp, PD, T, MNBA, FHsoc, AS Her cat actually was Christof Tourenski Mhp, PD, T, MNBA, FHsoc, AS.

Laura thought back to the websites advertising the qualifications. The study options. Self-study. Self-certification. In other words, you could take the course, ignore the learning material, and just declare yourself a graduate, with, if you wished it, honours. Grandad's implication was clear. To develop, manufacture, and prescribe alternative medicine you needed precisely and exactly no qualification, no accreditation, and no knowledge.

The qualifications which she'd seen displayed in Granny Gryene's office, and in the surgery of Barry the homeopath were doctorates a cat could be awarded. The certificate which Granny Gryene had been advocating Laura to take as a professional qualification was, in fact, achievable even if you lacked a basic understanding of anatomy, the power of speech, and opposable thumbs.

Grandad's sense of humour clearly had not left him.

Laura felt cheated. Had Grandad really created Christof's entire colourful history and applied for his bogus qualifications just to settle one of his tiffs with Granny Gryene? There must be more.

Chapter 11: Empty Vessels

"I'd like to see Granny. " She stopped herself, "Sylvia Gryene," she said. The woman behind the desk smiled condescendingly.

"Ms. Gryene is a very busy woman" she said.

"Tell her it's her granddaughter," persisted Laura. The woman smiled as though everybody asking for a meeting without an appointment gave her that story.

"I'll try," she said, "if you want to wait." She went back to her computer.

Laura did not want to wait. Laura had some questions to ask Granny Gryene. The most significant of which was why her cat was more highly qualified than her high-flying grandmother. She looked at the security gate. Right next to it was the toilet door. She made for the toilet, and went inside. Through a crack in the door, she waited until the receptionist had turned her back, then slipped out, and hopped the gate.

It would not, she thought, be safe to cross the factory floor, so she skirted around, dodging from pillar to pillar. Work was going on just as before. The sea of pills. The enticing colours. The tumble dryer of medications. Laura kept out of site and made her way through the complex towards Sylvia Gryene's office.

In the corridors of the office building, she was completely exposed. A woman appeared suddenly from a lift, but there was nowhere to hide. Laura stared straight ahead and kept walking. The woman smiled and nodded to her as she passed, but said nothing.

Finally, she approached the door of Sylvia Gryene's office. From inside, she could hear a man's voice. There was something familiar about it. She paused. The door opened suddenly, and Laura flung herself through the next door along and slammed it after her. She peered out through the glass window. Her instinct had been right. It was the cat killer! What was he doing here?

She watched him walk right by her door, and away.

"Can I help you, miss?" said a voice from behind her. She spun around. A slightly pointy man in a crumpled suit was watching her from behind a pair of half-moon glasses.

"Sorry," she said, "wrong office." Before he could say anything else, she smiled and left the room.

"Who was that man?" Laura burst into Granny Gryene's office and confronted her.

"Laura?"

"Who was he?" she repeated.

"Marcus Yolandi," Sylvia Gryene said, surprised, "He's one of our best customers, a lovely man," she added, "and a great humanitarian."

"Really?" Laura must have sounded incredulous. He didn't seem like a humanitarian when he'd been pointing a gun at her.

"Yes, he does great work in Uganda," she said.

"What kind of work?"

"What's this about?" said Granny Gryene.

"I saw him at the funeral," said Laura quickly. Her mind spinning.

"He was a friend of your grandad's. I introduced them as a matter of fact," She looked suddenly sad, "I thought maybe

Marcus could help him." She shook her head. "Is this about your grandad?"

"He tried to kill my cat," said Laura.

"What are you talking about?" said Granny Gryene, "Laura, why are you here?"

"Is he coming back?" she asked.

"In a minute," she said. "I'll introduce you."

"I have to go." said Laura, abruptly. She turned and left the still shocked Sylvia Gryene, slamming the door after her. The questions would have to wait.

At the end of the corridor, she heard footsteps. Marcus Yolandi appeared around the corner. He was staring down at his mobile, poking the screen. Laura dived at the other end of the corridor, and through a set of double swing doors.

She did not stop to see if she had been spotted, but instead careered blindly around the next corner where she collided with a thin man in a white coat.

He stopped, brushed himself down and grinned at her.

"You again?" said Laura.

"Me again," said Dr. Dan Pan, brightly.

"How did you get in?" Laura hissed.

"I have a white coat," said Dr. Dan. "A white coat will get you into pretty much anywhere." He paused, "Except an operating theatre. You need a green coat for that."

"What are you doing here?"

"I'm following the cat killer. He's here," said Dr. Dan.

"I know - his name is Marcus Yolandi," she whispered, "I think he killed Grandad."

"It's not as simple as that," said Dr. Dan

"I know who Christof is."

"Congratulations," said Dr. Dan.

"What I don't understand is why?" she said.

"Let me take you on a tour of the factory," said Dr. Dan.

"I've already been around it," she said, "I'm going to be taking it over."

If she'd hoped this would impress him, it didn't. He looked suddenly serious. "Then I think you'd better have a look around with me first," he said. He walked briskly off through a set of doors, and onto the factory floor. Laura followed, gingerly.

"Come on." All over the room, people were working. They could be spotted at any second, but Dr. Dan seemed unconcerned.

"We're not supposed to be here!" Laura hissed, hanging back.

"White coat - remember!" said Dr. Dan, flashing his smile, "I'm allowed everywhere."

She crept nervously after him. He seemed to be right. People looked up at them as they passed, shrugged and got on with their work.

"Oh, look - homeopathic are such fun!" said Dr. Dan as he lead her over to the big vat containing the virgin unprocessed pills Granny Gryene had shown her on her first visit. "Notice anything odd? He said?"

Laura didn't. Dr. Dan picked up a handful of pills and opened his mouth. Laura gasped, and grabbed his arm. Too late. He shoved the pills into his mouth and crunched on them.

"What are you doing?" she asked, horrified.

"What's the matter - worried about side effects?" he said, spitting pills out in all directions, "These drugs have no side effects, remember."

"OK," said Laura - still unsure.

"What's the problem? Come on, you know the answer - what's the problem?" Laura felt like she was being quizzed. There was something disturbing about watching a trusted TV doctor stuffing his mouth with pills without a care in the world.

"I -" she started, "I thought all drugs had side effects."

"Right!" said Dr. Dan, "all drugs have side effects!"

"Ah!" said Laura, "but these are just blanks" Granny Gryene had used the word 'blanks'. "The active drug gets sprayed onto them later."

"That's right!" said Dr. Dan. "Now I wonder why that is. Why not just stick it in the pill? Makes more sense, don't you think? Well, let's go and see that, shall we?"

He bundled her away, pausing only to spit out the remaining dry pills. They hurried across the factory floor until they reached the huge pill dryer with its rolling, tumbling wheel of tablets. As before, there was a man spraying the active ingredient onto the tablets. He barely took any notice as the two stood behind him watching.

"So what's going on here?" Dr. Dan asked Laura.

"The drug is in the liquid. They're spraying it onto the pills, and then drying them." she said.

"Right," said Dr. Dan, "mixing it up as a liquid, spraying on and then drying it off again. Sounds a bit of a palaver, doesn't it? Still, never mind that. Must be pretty powerful, concentrated stuff."

"I guess," said Laura.

"So why isn't he wearing a mask?" He looked at the man with the spray gun, and then at Laura. She shrugged. "Seriously? In here, all day, every day spraying away. He must breathe in gallons of the stuff. Bit of a health risk, don't you think?"

"I suppose so."

"Well, we'd better find out what this mysterious elixir is, hadn't we?" said Dr. Dan. "If only for the sake of this poor man's health!" Dr. Dan strode off. Laura followed, a little unsettled.

Dr. Dan led her off the production line, and down corridors. Every time they came to a door, opened it, peered inside and then closed it again, apologising to the occupants.

"Not that one," he kept muttering to himself.

Eventually, they came to a glass door. Dr. Dan opened it and slipped inside, beckoning Laura after him. She'd seen this room on her last visit, but only in passing. It was filled with scientific instruments, and particularly with glass containers containing solutions of different liquids. They ranged from dark, deep colours through to utterly transparent liquids.

The scientists within barely looked up from their work as the two entered.

"This is the nerve centre of the operation," Dr. Dan whispered in sarcastic awe, "It's where they concentrate the remedies." Dr. Dan pointed to the rows of liquids. "This is a headache remedy - I saw your mother taking one at the funeral." he said, "They're fairly common. Lots of people use them. But which ones are the most concentrated?" he asked. She pointed at the first small jar. It was dark, deep purple in colour, completely opaque, and thick like treacle.

"That one," she said.

"You'd think, wouldn't you?" smiled Dr. Dan. "But no." he tapped the biggest jar. It was full of liquid so clear it looked like air. "Let's see how this stuff is made, shall we?" He pointed at the purple jar, then beckoned her through into another room. It contained rows of plastic vats. Into each one, a technician was feeding branches of plants. As Laura watched, the man picked up a big handful of dark purple berries and flowers, and dumped them into a vat, pressing them down into the liquid. At the bottom of the vat, a small tap dripped the same dark, almost black liquid she'd seen in the other room into a small jar.

"What do you notice?" asked Dr. Dan.

Laura looked at the man. "He's wearing gloves," she said. In fact, he was wearing a full protective suit and a mask as well.

"Right. That's a bit odd, don't you think? Considering this is just the un-concentrated version and the guy spraying the really concentrated stuff didn't have any protective gear at all?"

"So this stuff cures headaches?" said Laura. Dr. Dan laughed.

"God no!" he said, darkly, "That stuff is belladonna. Otherwise known as deadly nightshade. The clue is in the name."

"It's poisonous?"

"Deadly."

"So..." Laura was starting to feel a bit foolish, "how does that cure headaches?"

"It doesn't," said Dr. Dan, plainly enjoying himself, "It gives you headaches. Headaches, delirium, hallucinations, rashes, dizziness, convulsions, and then death." The list of ailments tripped off his tongue as though he was listing the range of sweets in a pick and mix. "It's one of the most poisonous plants on earth. Two berries can be enough to kill." Dr. Dan paused.

"My mum takes that most days," said Laura.

"One of the ideas of homeopathy is that if something makes you ill, it will also cure you."

"Have they tried it with gunshot wounds?" said Laura. "Maybe the assassin was trying to cure me." In her pocket, Laura fingered the box of pills she had been given for her food poisoning. She remembered the name stamped on the side: 'Arsenicum', as in arsenic. She'd assumed that was just a trade name. She began to feel a little queasy again. "Is this what Grandad meant when he said he'd been murdered? Are the tablets poisonous?"

"No. If they were poison, everyone would know. What this stuff does is worse than poison."

"What does it do?"

"Nothing." said Dr. Dan. Laura looked puzzled. Dr. Dan went on, "It gets stranger. You see that stuff?" He pointed at the thick drops of liquid poison dropping slowly from the tap at the bottom of the vat. "That could kill thousands, but that's not the concentrated stuff. Shall we see how they concentrate it?"

Laura nodded. He lead her back through the glass door, and they watched as another technician took the bottle of deadly nightshade reduction, and, with a pipette, dripped a single drop into a large jar of clear liquid. The drop exploded downwards in an inverted mushroom cloud, expanding and dissipating into the liquid. Slowly, the purple faded until the thick jar was clear again.

"What's in there?" whispered Laura.

"Water," said Dr. Dan, "just water."

The technician sealed the top of the jar, carried it carefully over to a table on which a soft, leather cushion sat. He lifted the jar slowly, and brought it down hard on the cushion. There was a soft thud, and a gurgle of water. The technician raised the jar again, and brought it down. He repeated the procedure several times in a slow, practiced way. It was almost like a religious ritual.

"Now watch," said Dr. Dan.

The technician returned the bottle to the first table, opened it, and used another pipette to take a drop from it, and drip it into another large jar of water. This time, there was no mushroom cloud. No slowly dispersing ribbon of dark liquid. Just one clear drop in a clear jar. The technician sealed it, and took it over to the leather pillow for another slow session of ritual impacts. Dr. Dan watched, smiling. The technician returned, opened the bottle, and took another single drop which he placed into yet another bottle of water.

"What is this?" whispered Laura, "surely it's just water by now!"

"Oh, yes." said Dr. Dan, "Homeopaths think that the more you dilute the solution, the stronger it gets,"

"OK," said Laura.

"They think the water remembers what it's had in it."

Laura blinked at him. She knew that water had been around for as long as the planet had. If water had a memory, it would probably, by now, have quite a lot of chemical memory to store in its runny mind - and most of it would be of seaweed and dinosaur poo.

"So how much poison is in the tablets?" she asked.

"Well," said Dr. Dan, "if they're really strong, they're labelled 30c - that means to drink one molecule of poison, you'd have to drink all the water on Earth several times over."

"So the guy with the spray didn't need protective clothing because he was just spraying water?" said Laura. Dr. Dan smiled. "And the pills don't have any side effects because there's nothing in them - except this 'memory' thing in the water?"

"Yes," said Dr. Dan, "except that if the guy with the spray was just spraying water, and the pills when you get them are dry, then that means - "

"- that even the water is gone by the time they sell them." Laura said.

"But it works!" she said, "Judy takes it for her headaches - I took some yesterday for food poisoning. If it's such a load of rubbish, how come it works?"

"We'll get to that," said Dr. Dan pointedly, "but first..."

"Excuse me, but who are you?" one of the lab-coated technicians had finally noticed them standing in the corner watching. "Only, this is a closed area."

"Quite right too!" said Dr. Dan. "We were just – um" He grinned broadly at the man, then ushered Laura out of the room, and set off purposefully down the corridor. They turned left, and then right, and then right again. Eventually she stopped him.

"You don't know where you're going, do you?" she said.

"Not a clue." he admitted, "but I think the white coat disguise is probably not going to get us much further. I think it's time we left."

Laura thought for a moment. They could go straight to Granny Gryene and demand an explanation, but Laura wasn't completely sure what she would be demanding an explanation for just yet, and in any case, there was definitely one murderer in, or near, her office, and Laura had just seen enough poison to take out a small town. Leaving the factory as quickly and quietly as possible, and chatting things over in a coffee shop with Dr. Dan seemed like the best option, all things considered.

They couldn't go out the way she'd come in. The woman at reception might be clueless, but it would have occurred to her by now that Laura hadn't spent the last hour in the toilet. The factory floor was closed from the outside, and the labs only opened into the main building.

On her way in, she'd seen lorries being loaded. A big doorway opened into a warehouse. That was their best chance. She grabbed Dr. Dan's arm and led him back the way they had come. If she remembered right, the warehouse should be on the other side of the factory floor. As they stepped out into the factory, Laura noticed two security guards. One spotted them immediately, and shouted.

Laura grabbed Dr. Dan's hand and they ran, dodging between vats of pills. She realised they had no chance of making it all the way across the factory, through the warehouse, and out of the complex without getting caught. They sprinted past the pill-churning machine with its attendant still spraying highly concentrated water pointlessly onto the pills, and Laura almost lost her balance, skidding on the wet floor. As she passed, she grabbed a wheel on the side of the mixer, turning the whole machine and tipping the tiny pills over the floor behind them.

Laura glanced back. The Guards skated into the wet tablets, their legs flailing. They held onto each other to steady themselves. Laura and Dr. Dan ran on.

Up ahead, a long conveyor belt blocked their way. It stretched all the way across the factory floor to their right, disappearing through a hatch into the wall on the far side. They veered left, with the guards recovering and giving chase behind them, and past a large metal arch covering the belt.

From inside, there was the rattling sound of pills being sorted. Laura grabbed a safety bar on the side of the arch as they passed, and used it to swing herself up and onto the belt. Dr. Dan followed.

The belt itself held her weight, buckling just slightly, and stuttering to a halt, but as she leapt off onto the floor on the other side, it jerked forward suddenly, twisting her foot out from under her. She landed badly, twisting her ankle, but the guards stopped at the belt. Not willing to risk climbing on the machines, they took the long way around.

Dr. Dan pulled her to her feet. Pain shot through her leg. She forced herself to walk, and then run on the wounded ankle, and they stumbled off the factory floor, and into the warehouse. In front of them, a cityscape of stacked boxes and palettes.

Dr. Dan pulled Laura between two tall columns of crates. She crouched down, her leg burning in pain.

"Wait here," he said, "I'll find the way out and come back for you." He disappeared, and she heard his footsteps across the floor. Suddenly, she heard a shout, and the footsteps stopped abruptly. She dragged herself to the corner of her pile of boxes and peered out.

A few meters away, Marcus Yolandi had Dr. Dan pinned against the wall. His face, dark and angry. Behind him, Granny Gryene stood, looking baffled. Laura sank back behind the crates. Now what?

The line of boxes extended right along the side of the warehouse, forming a narrow corridor. If she got a little closer, she might be able to at least hear the conversation. She crept along the boxes as quietly as she could. As her injured foot touched the floor, she winced silently, wondering what a homeopathic twisted ankle remedy might contain.

When she got as close as she could, she peered out through a crack between the boxes. She could see Dr. Dan struggling helplessly. Yolandi was holding him by the neck against the wall.

"What do you know? What do you know?" he kept repeating. Dr. Dan was making strangled noises.

"Marcus, leave him. What are you doing?" protested Sylvia Gryene. Then, she squinted at Dr. Dan, "I know you! You're Dan Pan!" Dr. Dan tried to nod.

Yolandi growled at her, "You were at the funeral - you heard him say we had killed him."

"Oh, Marcus - he didn't mean us!" she said incredulously, "it was just one of his silly games!"

"No," said Yolandi, "I saw him before he died. He planned to punish us."

"What are you talking about? For what? And in any case, what could he do? He was dying!" Granny Gryene's voice was cracking. She looked, to Laura, as though she had no more idea what was going on than Laura herself did.

"You do not know the dying," said Yolandi, darkly, "The dying are the most dangerous of men. They are willing to play all their cards at one time." He paused. "It has something to do with the girl and her cat - that's all I know."

"What cat?" Granny Gryene stopped, suddenly her voice changed, "Do you mean my granddaughter?"

Laura edged closer to the corner of the boxes. She looked around. Leaning against the fire extinguisher on the wall was a large hammer. Maybe if she could grab it she could throw it at Yolandi. It didn't seem like a good plan, but it was all she had.

"I've taken care of the cat," said Yolandi grimly. "This man tried to stop me - he must know something." Dr. Dan made a choking noise. Yolandi loosened his grip a little.

"You killed the wrong cat," gasped Dr. Dan.

"My granddaughter has nothing to do with this - whatever it is!" Granny Gryene shouted. Then she paused, "You killed her cat?"

"He killed the wrong cat," said Dr. Dan.

"You will tell me what all this is about!" Yolandi's voice was threatening. Unpredictable. He could do anything, Laura thought. She crept forward. The hammer was nearly within her grasp. She crouched, and sprang towards it, hoping that her half-formed plan would come together once she grabbed the weapon.

What happened was that somewhere in mid leap, she changed her plan. She landed, pushed the hammer out of the way, and grabbed the fire extinguisher instead. In one movement, she spun round, pulled the pin out, and squeezed the trigger, pointing the nozzle at Marcus Yolandi.

A cloud of CO_2 instantly engulfed all four of them. Laura pushed forwards, grabbing Dr. Dan and pulling him on through the thick cloud of gas. She waved the nozzle, wildly, spreading clouds in all directions, and the two sprinted towards the exit of the building.

They were almost at the door, when suddenly, Marcus Yolandi exploded out of the billowing cloud behind them, grabbed Dr. Dan round the waist and he crashed to the ground.

"Run!" Dr. Dan shouted, and without looking back, Laura sprinted, ignoring the pain in her leg, out of the giant door, around the parked lorries, through the open gates of the factory, and into the evening.

Chapter 12: Night With The Living Dead

Sitting on a park bench in the dark, Laura felt around her ankle. It was swollen and still painful, but the ache was beginning to die down. She tried rotating her foot. It could do with a couple of days rest, she decided. The chances of it getting a couple of days rest were pretty low. Laura suspected she would be doing a lot more running before Grandad's little game was over.

Laura pulled out her phone and hit the spreadsheet app. "LIST" she typed. Then underneath, "PEOPLE I CAN TRUST".

Laura paused for a long time. Eventually, she typed "Grandad." In the next cell along, she wrote, "DEAD". She thought for a while, then in the next row, she typed "Dr. Dan Pan." Next to his name, "PROBABLY DEAD". A pattern was beginning to emerge.

In her mind, she ran through a few more people. Peter and Judy, Granny Gryene, Mrs. Blythe. None of them seemed to be worth adding to the list. She glanced back at it. Two names. Both out of the picture. She couldn't help feeling a little lonely.

Samuel popped into her head for some reason she could not quite get her head around. She probably could trust him in the sense that he was too much of an idiot to be involved in any plots, but his obsession with guns pretty much excluded him from the list.

There was, of course one more name she could add. It was a bit sad for a teenage girl, she thought, and she hesitated before typing, "Christof Tourenski" on the next line down. For disambiguation, she added, in brackets, "CAT." A non-human confidant, she felt, was marginally better than a completely fictional one. Especially such an active, and unpredictable piece of fiction as the real, fake, Christof Tourenski was turning out to be.

She couldn't sleep at home tonight. That much was clear. Yolandi probably knew where she lived, and Sylvia Gryene certainly did. Sylvia didn't seem completely on the same page as her "humanitarian" friend with his murderous rampages, but she was certainly off her granddaughter's "people to trust" list for now.

Laura looked at her pitiful list again. Christof was at home right now, and if only to preserve at least one of the listed individuals on the mortal plane, she would have to go and get him.

Everyone on Laura's street had their own driveway. No parking on the road. So why was there a dark car sitting on the double yellow lines opposite her house? She felt a sick feeling in her stomach as she ducked into the garden at the end of the street, and started to pick her way from house to house in the shadows.

She got closer and closer to the unfamiliar car, but the lights inside were off. She couldn't tell whether someone was inside, watching her house, or whether it was just badly parked. It wasn't worth taking the risk.

She limped over the low fence between the two houses opposite her parents' and crept across the neat lawn of Mary Dickens' house to peer through the hedge at the car. Mary was doubtless tucked up in bed right now wearing a pink toweling onesie.

She and Laura had lived opposite each other for their entire lives, yet Laura had never had any interest in her frilly, girly games, or her goody-goody attitude, or her prim and proper parents. This was the first time in her life she had stepped on their perfect lawn and it felt like enemy territory.

As her feet touched the gravel of the driveway, she was suddenly blinded. The automatic security light highlighted her frozen figure, right in front of the window of the dark car.

Instantly, the door flew open and out stepped Mary Dickens. Her cheeks were flushed and her hair was messy. The remains of red lipstick was smudged on her mouth. She looked back into the car where a sheepish, slightly older boy was sitting. He leant over, shut the door, and drove off.

"I won't tell if you don't," she said, quietly, and crept around the house to the back door.

Laura sighed, crossed the road, and went inside.

In the living room, her parents were sitting in silence. She could tell instantly that something was wrong. Peter was back to his old, slumped self. Judy sat next to him, hands on her knees, doing her breathing exercise. In through the mouth, hold for three, and out through the nose. Over and over. She only ever did it in situations where no amount of meditation or centred mindfulness was ever going to help.

"Sit down," she said, "Peter and I have something to tell you. It may come as a shock."

It didn't come as a shock. It came as the absolute complete opposite of a shock. Judy slowly and carefully and sympathetically explained to Laura that it was very likely that the cat's home would have to close.

She explained that they had tried their very best to rescue the situation, and that they had tried their very best to shield Laura from the worry that they had been going through, but that they had tried everything, and now the summons had been issued. The hearing was in a couple of days, and all hope was extinguished.

"We've tried to put a brave face on it for you, Laura," Judy explained, "but there comes a time when we all have to face the truth. We feel," she said, "as though you are mature enough to understand."

There was a part of her which wanted to leap in the air and shout "Hallelujah!" Finally, the penny had dropped. Finally, after all these months, her parents had, by some miracle, come into momentary contact with the real world!

Laura's eyes filled. Not through sadness, but through pure relief. She choked back the desire to grab her mother by the throat and scream that this is what she had been trying to tell them for months. That if only they'd listened to her months ago, all this could have been avoided. She wanted to run to her room, and grab the pages of spreadsheets she'd printed out and carefully explained to her parents over and over again for the last four years, and force them to eat them.

Instead, she gritted her teeth, and said "Oh, dear."

"You do understand what this means?" Judy said, "The cats may have to be -" She couldn't continue. Instead, she breathed in very slowly counting to three, and then out again. Laura looked at her, then at Peter, sagging into the sofa. She really should stay with them, but she couldn't. Not tonight.

"I'm going out tonight," said Laura, heading for the stairs, "I'm staying over with friends," She said it as casually as she could, adding, "If Granny Gryene calls, tell her I'll see her soon."

Christof was waiting in the bedroom, asleep. She clipped his lead on, grabbed a change of clothes, pulled the gun out from under her bed and shoved it into her bag, picked up Christof, and headed for the door.

"Laura?" Peter was filling the doorway of the lounge, like a melting yeti.

"Yes?" she said.

"Promise me you'll come to the hearing," he said. "It's the day after tomorrow."

"Of course, Dad," she said. The word, Dad took them both by surprise as it came out of her mouth, "Of course I will!" She stepped outside, checked the road for suspicious cars, and hurried away.

There was only one place she could go. Actually, there were two places, but she wasn't going to ask Samuel for a bed for the night. Even though she was armed, that wasn't going to happen.

It would have to be the cat sanctuary. The office window was open to the street, so she left the light off, and crept past its piles of unfiled paperwork, which would now never be filed. The forms and vets bills and documents would all soon be incinerated, as would the bodies of the cats they referred to. Living rubbish.

She and Christof slunk past. The definition of cat burglars.

Kennington Paws was different at night. It was more alive, more active. Eyes, white in the torchlight, paced back and forth. Conversations were conducted. Differences settled. Territories were marked and defended. With Gordon Ramsey dead, and Delia Smith gone to replace an electrified sister, Nigella Lawson sat alone. Queen of all she surveyed.

Laura looked into her fiery face. Without her adversaries she was somehow diminished. Less noble. More saleable, Laura thought, as if that mattered now.

Roland Rat still cowered in the corner of his cage, as though the ghosts of the inseparable Chuckle Brothers still prowled, constantly pressed against each other, like some conjoined insect-cat. But the Siamese twins had gone now to be parents to an orphan. Roland had nothing to fear now, but still he cowered. Sometimes, thought Laura, your enemies defined you as much as your friends.

The séance had unbalanced the dynamic and missing cats meant everyone had to reassess their relationships. Laura looked for a comfortable spot to lie down on the cold, stale concrete floor. With the smell of cat urine, and disinfectant, dark and acid, she was reassessing hers too.

There was, needless to say, no comfortable place to lie on the pitted floor. There was also little chance of sleep with the cats working out their differences around her. Christof Tourenski strode back and forth along the lines of cages, inspecting each in turn. He was clearly enjoying his position as, not only the most qualified, but also, the only uncaged animal in the room. The other residents took turns to sneer at him for his favoured status.

Laura propped herself up against the door - sitting on the cold floor was a degree less uncomfortable than lying on it - and watched him, hoping that sleep would overtake her. It didn't. Her mind was moving too fast to be overtaken by anything.

She was stuck in another loop - asking herself where Dr. Dan could be, which side Sylvia Gryene was on, and why it had suddenly become her job to know, over and over, as though she was a talking toy with just those three phrases.

Every few minutes, the exhaustion of repeating the same unanswered questions in her head allowed her to slip into a sort of drowsiness which was not sleep. Her head nodded forwards onto her chest. She closed her eyes. Then after a time which could have been a minute, an hour or an instant, the sudden screech, or hiss of a cat, or the twang of claws against wire bars jerked her back to full wakefulness, growing angrier and more frustrated each time.

Finally, she couldn't take it any longer. She leaped to her feet, and screamed at the cats, "Shut up! Shut up! SHUT UP!" She clenched her fists, and tore at her hair. She stamped on the hard floor until sharp pains shot through her feet, and she balled into the cages at the top of her voice.

The silence that followed lasted about a second and a half before the cats' attention switched away from her, and they went back to their screeching, fighting, and pacing as though nothing had happened. Laura, sobbing, sank against the door, and slid down to the floor, her fists pressed hard against her ears.

She had no idea how long it was before her eyes began to close, and she felt the darkness swimming in around her, but in the end, her head nodded forward again, and she felt the muscles in her arms relax, and flop.

She was woken by another screech. This time, very close. As she jerked into wakefulness, her eyes flew open, and were instantly blinded by a flash from her lap, and she felt a cat leap past her face.

She shook her head, and her vision cleared. Somehow, Christof had jumped onto her tablet, hit the photo button, and taken a picture as he'd leaped up onto her shoulder. She stared in horror as the screen came into focus. It was perfectly composed. On one side, Christof's bum-hole, blurring away from the camera. On the other, Laura, wide eyed, shocked and vacant. Her hair wild. Her mouth slightly open, the harsh light of the tablet's flash, whiting out her skin.

And the bizarre thing. The yawningly terrible, horrifying thing about the wild, sleep-deprived, mad-girl selfie staring back at her from the tablet screen?

She realised that she was OK with it.

It looked right. It looked like Laura. It wasn't the windswept heroine she'd wanted to see herself as at Grandad's funeral, or the smart business brain she'd tried to channel in Granny Gryene's office, or even the sulky daughter caricature she put on for her parents. But it was right. The strange woman with the cat on her shoulder and the dark rimmed eyes was, undeniably, Laura. Probably the first - no, she thought, definitely - the first picture of herself she'd ever actually been happy with.

It was a revelation. In that second, she finally recognised herself. She was one of the Cat People. The bizarre misfits of the world she'd observed and suddenly found a name for at Ms. Blythe's séance. She had told herself that she would always recognise those unique souls when she saw them. And looking at the screen now, she saw herself.

Not one of *Ms. Blythe's* cat people, certainly. She wasn't a nutter! But there was Laura, staring back at herself. A Cat Person, and Christof Tourenski, her cat. When all this was over, Laura decided, that shot would be her Facebook profile picture.

And with that thought came another. Dr. Dan Pan was on her side, but he was unlikely to have been acting alone. And there was one other person she had seen him with: Melvin Rochester.

They had been talking secretly together at the funeral. Then later at the TV studio, Rochester had thought that Laura was present as part of some plan. And a plan there had to be. If Christof Tourenski was not a real person, then that raised its own issues. Somebody was, even now, promoting his growing fame across the land. It seemed likely that Rochester knew who that was, or had his suspicions.

It was worth a shot. She flicked open her tablet, tapped his name in and began to pick through the thousands of search results.

By the time, she found him, the small window in the corner had turned from London's streetlamp yellow to a dull grey, and finally to the brighter grey that signified morning when the cats began to quieten.

Finally, she found what she was looking for. In a small side-bar on one of the national news sites, there was a mention of Rochester. He was going to be at the Houses of Parliament in the morning, giving undoubtedly scathing testimony to the government's inquiry into alternative medicine. Perhaps if she could catch him on the way in, she might be able to find out what he really knew. Maybe he would know where the "humanitarian" assassin might have taken Dr. Dan.

Laura leapt up, clipped Christof's lead on and hefted her bag onto her shoulder. It felt hard and heavy. She stopped. Probably, if she were planning a visit to the country's legislative seat, she thought, it might be wise *not* to take the gun with her. She could think of a number of uses for it inside the building, but she couldn't help feeling things might get distractingly official if she tried to gain entry with it.

She slipped the gun out of her bag, opened one of the cages, and tucked the weapon under the Boston Strangler's bedding. She would have to come back for it, but it gave her a little satisfaction to think of the kitten making a last stand against the vet with his bag of poisoned needles. Of course, the little kitten would have to find a work-around for his lack of an opposable thumb.

She looked quickly around the cages, nodded a grim acknowledgement to her night-time companions.

"Goodbye, cats," she said out loud, and slipped out of the room.

Chapter 13: Fame And Fortune Tellers

There are places in the world where the appearance of a minor celebrity can stop traffic. Where a singer with a fleeting hit, or a TV presenter in a headscarf can cause roads to be blocked and throngs of autograph hunters to spontaneously coalesce out of the crowds, camera phones held high to snatch a blurred snapshot for social media. London, and especially, Parliament Square, in the shadow of Big Ben and the houses of parliament is one such place.

There are also places where a hugely important figure - a government minister, for example, or a member of royalty, or an eminent scientist - can pass by, recognised by all, but unremarked. London, and especially Parliament Square, is that sort of place as well.

As Laura stood in front of the big arch through which people funneled into the building, she spotted several faces she had seen being interviewed on news programmes, and several others, hovering nearby, who she'd seen interviewing them. The reporters seemed to know who to pester for interviews, and who to allow to pass unmolested.

Perhaps, she thought, the secret was in the way you walked. If you walked as though you wanted to be spotted, then spotted you were. If you walked as though you had places to go, and stuff to do, the reserved folk of England, the tourists staring in awe from one London monument to the next, and even the hovering celebrity journalists picked up on the cue, and left you alone.

Whatever the cues were, Laura had not mastered them. As a cat walker, tourists apparently found her more photo-worthy than the government ministers filing into work behind her. She tried to ignore the attention and concentrate on looking out for Melvin Rochester. However, from across the green, where the TV cameras and seasoned journalists were lined up waiting for their interviewees, Laura suddenly spotted another familiar face - or rather, a familiar mask. It was the horribly over-made-up face of Christof expert, Josephine Gilliam. Laura quickly stepped in front of Christof, but it was too late. She saw the woman stare at her for a second, turn to the journalist she was chatting to and point. In seconds, the whole gaggle were hoisting up their microphones and marching over towards her.

It must, she thought, be a slow news day. Laura turned and at that moment, she saw the figure of Melvin Rochester heading towards the entrance. She sprinted after him, dragging Christof behind her on the lead.

Damn. Even if she caught him now, she could hardly ask the questions she needed to ask in front of the press. She ran anyway, shouting to him, but it was too late. He disappeared inside the building without looking back.

Without thinking, Laura dived in after him.

"Can I help you, Miss?" said the big security guard in a voice that implied the kind of help he was offering would not be welcomed by anybody.

Laura paused for a moment and then smiled as broadly as she could.

"Yes!" she said, "Just coming in to - ah - "the security guard had a very expressive face. He communicated, with practiced ease, the fact that he was going to insist that she finish her sentence, and finish it in a truly impressive way before he would allow her to pass.

Laura hesitated and hopped from foot to foot. Christof looked up at the man. This was not going well.

Suddenly a smaller security guard popped her head out from behind the larger one. She looked Laura and Christof up and down, then through the door at the crowd of grinning TV presenters thrusting their microphones through.

"It's the Cat Girl!" she said to her companion. "George, it's the Cat Girl." George's expressive face offered up puzzlement. She turned to Laura, "You're in the wrong place, dear," she said.

"Am I?" said Laura.

"You're Christof Tourenski's spokeswoman, aren't you?" Laura nodded, trying to look less puzzled than George. "You're on my list for the College Garden reception. Did you bring your invite, dear?" Laura shook her head, "Not to worry, I'll take you over! It can be so confusing, can't it?"

"Yes," said Laura, "definitely."

The woman grabbed her elbow and led her out through the crowd of journalists, singing, "just ignore them, dear," as she guided her, across the road, "I saw you on the telly. I am such a fan! You made mincemeat of that Rochester. Odious man! Tell me," she said, "What's Christof really like? They say he never speaks." Laura looked down at her cat.

"I've never known him to," she said.

"How do you communicate?"

"Oh, we manage," said Laura, "I sort of speak on his behalf."

"How exciting," she said.

She lead Laura through a gate and up to another set of security guards, she smiled at them and said, "This is Christof Tourenski's spokeswoman! She's on your list." One of the guards checked his list, and nodded. He ticked off a name.

Obviously, she had been invited. Or Christof had. Laura remembered there had been an unopened pile of post in the hall as she'd left. Probably, the invite had been amongst that. It seemed Christof Tourenski's reputation was preceding him. By quite a long way.

"Just need to check your bags," the security guard said. Laura handed her bag over, "Just to check you're not carrying any guns!" he joked.

"I was earlier," Laura smiled back, "but I gave it to the Boston Strangler."

"In you go," said the guard. Laura took her bag, and she and Christof walked into a party for which she definitely was not appropriately dressed.

Everyone else in the high-walled garden was dressed in the kind of clothes you wore only to be photographed in. Brightly coloured dresses, smart suits, and hats. There were ribbons. There were clutch bags. There were polished shoes.

And between them, weaved waitresses carrying trays of miniaturised breakfasts. There were bite sized croissants and pain au chocolat, ornamental china spoons, each containing a single arrangement of artisan granola, or exotic fruit salad. And for the more traditional, there were fried English breakfasts, shrunk onto skewers - a delicate hash brown on the bottom, a disk of black pudding, a crispy spiral of bacon wrapped around a soft boiled quail's egg. Coffees and fruit juices occupied the hands of guests as they flitted and shifted in the smiling dance of eternal networking.

This was a party with a purpose, that was clear. People were ostentatiously behaving as though they knew each other well, which clearly meant that they didn't. Laura shifted uncomfortably and looked around for a clue about exactly what kind of breakfast club she had been invited to.

"Geraldine Hartley, Minister for Health." A woman in a blue woolen suit had launched herself at Laura from the crowd, her hand extended in what turned out to be an enthusiastic handshake, "So pleased to meet you, finally. I've been reading so much about your work -" she paused, "Or Christof's work, at least. I am so interested in what you do - what he does!" Laura felt vaguely disappointed. She never had much time for politicians, but she did feel that at some point, it would be right that her and her cat's obvious deception would be spotted. Hoodwinking the media was one thing, but surely the person in charge of health for the entire country should have been able to spot a blatant hoaxer when she saw one? Clearly not.

The minister continued to gush, "We hoped he might be here in person, but I suppose that's..." she faltered slightly, struggling to end the sentence. Laura couldn't imagine what the Minister for Health 'supposed' about the mythical Christof's use of her as a medium. She, like everyone else, seemed happy to take it on trust despite the fact that it made no sense at all to Laura.

"Now, I'm sure you know what this little party is all about," continued Hartley. Laura looked at her. It seemed like a good time to smile and nod. "The rally is on Saturday and I am absolutely delighted that Christof has agreed to speak at it personally. You'll be introducing him. We're expecting a good crowd. We've been building up to this for months. It's all organised. This is our chance to make a real difference!"

Laura nodded again. It seemed preferable to asking what they had been building up to for months, or how Christof had signaled his agreement, or, indeed, stating flat out that she had no intention whatsoever of introducing anyone at any rally regardless of how good or bad the crowd was.

"And this is your cat?" said the Minister.

Another smile and a nod. "Who are the other cats?" Laura asked. On opposite sides of the garden, two other cats were skulking. Neither looked happy.

Geraldine smiled, "The black one is Gladstone, the Treasury's cat. The one with the white chest is Palmerston, the foreign office cat." The two glared at each other from across the garden, slowly circling, "They hate each other." She paused. "Let me introduce you around."

Geraldine Hartley whisked Laura into the throng, whirling her from one introduction to the next. Here was the lead singer of the Ice Crystals. There was the president of the Affiliation of Crystal Healing Practitioners. Here was Britain's newest top model. There was the chair of the Chiropractic phrenologists' association. Here was the MP for Bosworth. There was the heir to the throne.

Laura did a lot of smiling and nodding and seemed to fit right in because everyone else was doing the same. Geraldine helped immensely by barely giving her a chance to wonder at each individual's strange set of absolutely earnest beliefs about auras or toxins, or the restorative power of flower extracts, before hurrying her on to the next.

A single press photographer had secured an invite to the event and was reveling in it. Constantly on the lookout for images that he might sell later to the papers, his spiky, angular form popped up constantly wherever Laura and her cat went. Each time he did, whoever Laura was talking to would drape an arm around her and drag her into a grinning pose as though they were best mates. Every twenty seconds, another brief and famous acquaintance would be made, sealed forever in a digital snapshot and then broken again.

Once, a man in a sharp, striped suit wanted to talk to her about "megavitamins". He seemed to be trying to quietly offer to pay her in return for saying nice things about them. Another lady kept peering around her as they talked, and making brushing movements with her hands which she eventually revealed was her way of smoothing out the electrical impulses in Laura's energy field. Laura did not say it, but she had the distinct impression that the lady had some work to do before either of their energy fields was restored to balance.

While they were talking, Christof had been pulling at his lead, uncomfortable with its restriction, he had started to weave it in circles in and out of Laura's legs, and around the woman, pulling the two closer together until they were standing so closely Laura could see the streaks of grey and white in her hair.

Laura untangled them, and extended the lead to its full length, and Christof wandered slowly away in the direction of the wall. By the time she looked back, the lady was gone into the crowd. Now she was fingering the impulses of an actor who had once played a doctor in a soap opera. He was listening enraptured. "Yes!" he was saying, "Yes, I did feel that". And as quickly as that, his descent into New Age pseudoscience had begun.

Laura watched for a moment, and then, suddenly, her attention was caught by a commotion over to her left. Half of the party had stopped talking, and had turned to stare at the courtyard wall. On the grass beside it, the two governmental cats, Gladstone and Palmerston were squaring up against each other. Gladstone was hissing, crouched low, with his mouth wide. Palmerston, a meter away, was pawing the air.

Laura recognised it instantly. Classic territorial stuff. The garden was clearly an area of dispute and neither cat was going to back down.

The photographer was crouched in the grass, having decided that this bit of conflict might serve as an illustration of tensions within government. If the shots were good, he would be able to sell them to all the papers along with some headline involving a "spat" between the treasury and foreign office.

Laura watched. This wasn't going to be pretty. The two cats crouched and then sprang at each other, tumbling in a hissing, gouging ball across the grass. Gladstone sank his teeth into Palmerston's neck. Palmerston responded by tearing at his opponent's stomach with his back legs.

The crowd winced. The photographer snapped.

The two cats parted for a second, as though propelled away from each other on springs. Each hit the ground and turned back towards his opponent, teeth bared ready to take the fight to the next level. In that instant, Christof rose up out of the grass between them. He hissed at Palmerston, and then at Gladstone. The two pampered ministerial thoroughbreds cowered. Happy to take on each other, they were like petulant children when confronted with the streetwise confidence of a rescue cat.

They backed down instantly. Christof nodded dismissively from one to the other, and then walked gracefully back to Laura's side, posing in the flashing light of the photographer's camera. Gladstone and Palmerston retreated. Christof owned the garden.

"I've been following Christof's work on the medicinal properties of turmeric," mumbled a voice from behind her which had the low, deep rumble of a lorry failing to start. She turned around. It was the Prince of Wales, "Following it with great interest," he paused. "Great interest."

"Excuse me," said Laura, urgently, and pushed past him, diving into the crowd. Much as she would have liked to have stayed and discussed curry flavourings with the prince, something at the entrance of the garden had caught her eye.

A late arrival was being checked through security, and lead out into the garden. Dressed in an immaculate, tailored suit and skirt, and with faultless makeup, it was Granny Gryene. Laura reeled Christof in on his lead, picked him up, and edged towards the Minister for Health.

Of course Sylvia Gryene would be there. It was a chance to promote her work - and whatever this rally they were planning was about, Granny would be in it up to her eyes. Laura peered through the crowd. At least Marcus Yolandi didn't seem to be with her.

Laura made it to Geraldine Hartley, but over her shoulder, she could see Granny Gryene advancing on the group. She had one chance.

"I wondered if you could do me a favour," she said quickly. "I had a bit of a run in with Melvin Rochester on TV a couple of days ago -"

"I saw it!" interrupted the minister, "I've always found the man quite impossibly arrogant! You put him in his place"

"Well, he's just over the road right now," said Laura.

"Yes," Hartley looked suddenly serious, "He's giving his evidence to this damned inquiry," she said. "The thing is going straight into my waste bin when I get it, but I can't stop it happening. Still, we've got some good photos from this little party, so hopefully we can bury the story with those..." Over the minister's shoulder, Granny Gryene was getting closer and closer.

"I thought," said Laura, "if we popped over now, I could surprise him coming out - I could clear up a couple of points with him."

She paused. Granny Gryene was almost at the group of partygoers now. She could spot her at any second. A wicked smile spread across Geraldine's face. "I'd love to see that." She looked around, and smiled. "Come on! Let's go!"

Chapter 14: The Real Christof Tourenski

Laura ignored the minister's attempted introduction, and simply said "Dr. Dan Pan has been kidnapped."

If Rochester didn't know anything, she would look like a fool, but she judged that it was probably a bit late for that anyway. Laura and the minister had gained entry to the building on her personal say-so. Animals were only permitted for medical reasons, so she had to gain special dispensation for Christof. Laura could tell that security were not convinced, but they didn't feel sufficiently confident to challenge the minister on the question of just what kind of affliction might require the assistance of a guide-cat.

Once inside, they made their way to dark, wood paneled corridor which linked Parliament's dozens of committee rooms. The corridor was lined with green leather benches separating carved stone doorways, giving the place an atmosphere somewhere between a church, and a railway station waiting room.

They had barely entered the corridor when a door half way down flew open and Rochester strode out, and Laura and the minister grabbed him immediately. His eyebrows had just enough time to register surprise by springing upwards before Laura mentioned Dr. Dan, and they flew back down again in grim concentration.

A dark expression crossed his face, and he grabbed Laura by the elbow and propelled her towards the nearest empty room. He opened the door.

"Inside!" he said to her, and she followed Melvin Rochester into the room. Geraldine Hartley stepped to follow her.

The Minister of health looked bemused. Laura smiled sweetly at her, and closed the door in her face. It felt good to finally be the source of confusion to someone else, rather than being the recipient of it.

Rochester dropped himself into the chair at the head of the long table.

"Well?" he said.

Laura hooked Christof's lead on a chair, and sat. Rochester didn't move. His face was serious, his eyes fixed. He could have been part of the furniture. Christof climbed instantly onto the table and sat too, staring back.

Laura explained the whole thing. The attack at the funeral, the fight in the car park. The visit to the factory and their attempted escape.

Rochester listened quietly, shaking his head. When she had finished, he said, "He's an idiot."

"He saved my life," she said.

"That may be," said Rochester, "but quite possibly he put you in greater danger."

"How?"

"Sylvia Gryene and Marcus Yolandi have him," he said.

"I don't think she has anything to do with it," said Laura, "she seemed pretty surprised by Yolandi"

"She's in it up to her neck," said Rochester dismissively.

"She's my grandmother."

"So what?" he said. "She's as guilty as he is!"

"I don't think so!" Said Laura, angrily.

"Then you don't know her very well!" said Rochester. "In any case, we have to assume that they now know everything he knows,"

"I wish I did" said Laura.

"Did he tell you to find me?" he said.

"No." said Laura.

"Well done," he said. "How much do you know?"

"How much do you know?" said Laura cagily.

"You can trust me," said Rochester.

"That's funny, because I can't trust anyone else," she said flatly, "I didn't get much sleep last night, someone's trying to kill me, and I've just spent the morning stuck in a wizard's convention, so the world is looking fairly mad to me right now, and I would appreciate some straight answers"

Melvin Rochester sighed, "You mean the garden party?" he said with the kind of resignation that can only come from living in a world full of idiots. Laura recognised the tone immediately. He leaned forward and put his head in his hands.

"Every time," he said. "It happens every time!"

"What does?" she said.

"This is what it looks like when science fights democracy," said Rochester, "Companies like Gryene's spend an awful lot of money trying to get people in power like your friend the minister for health on their side."

"Why?" said Laura.

Rochester took a deep breath. "Because every company who thinks they've got a flower remedy to cure arthritis or a crystal that stops diabetes or some other kind of fairy dust, wants to get it prescribed by doctors and hospitals. The moment they do, they can make a lot more money." He paused. "The only problem is, they need to prove their potions work. Once they do that, it doesn't matter how strange or exotic it sounds, the medical profession will adopt it and they can collect their big pile of money and their worldwide fame and their Nobel Prize at the door. It's as simple as that."

"But?" said Laura.

"But people like me are running this massive scientific conspiracy."

"You are?" said Laura.

"Oh, yes, "said Rochester, "you see, we have this little rule about what constitutes proof. We say it's not good enough to just come up with a grand theory about life energies and toxins and exotic substances, and flower petals, and then wheel out a few people who are willing to say they took it and felt better. We say it doesn't matter how many people believe something is true. You have to check. And this is very inconvenient for the likes of your evil grandmother."

"Stop saying that!" snapped Laura. She thought about the tablet that cured her food poisoning, and the pills that Judy took daily to stave off headaches. They worked, she had no doubt, but she'd seen the concentrations of arsenic and deadly nightshade that went into them.

Rochester continued, "But the thing about alternative medicines is that they sound right. They sound like they would work, and who knows, some of them maybe do. But unless you do rigorous tests, you'll never know."

"So what's all this about?" said Laura.

"They've got to her," said Rochester simply, "Geraldine Hartley wants to relax the rules about what treatments get funded. When she talks about patient choice, what she really means is giving people the treatments patients *think* will work rather than the ones that have been proven to work. Democracy Versus science. You see?"

"And you're trying to stop her?" said Laura.

"I've been fighting this my whole life." he said, wearily. "She can only do it if she can make it look like the public are in favour," he said. "We've managed to set up this inquiry. We'd hoped that an independent government inquiry into alternative medicine would be enough to head her off."

"It hasn't worked?"

"She just planned this celebrity garden party for the same day, and now that will be all they print in the papers."

"She's organising a rally," said Laura.

"That's her plan," said Rochester. "A massive public demonstration in front of the houses of parliament. It'll be national news. They've been planning for months. Representatives of every quack therapy and every half-baked theory will be descending on Parliament Square on Saturday."

"And on the back of that, she'll push through her proposals?" said Laura.

"Yes."

"She wants me to speak at it," said Laura. "Me and Christof."

Rochester smiled, "I very much hope you will," he said, "We've pulled a lot of strings to get you up there."

"Not a chance!" Cried Laura.

Rochester paused, as though unsure whether to go on, then he said, "We needed to play them at their own game, and your grandfather gave us a way."

"I'm not doing it!" She said. "If people think crystals cure hay fever, then so what?" she thought of Bernard and his wonky knees, then she thought of Grandad. It wasn't as if ordinary medicine worked most of the time anyway. At least Granny's pills had made her feel better. "What's the harm?" she said.

"I have something I need to show you," said Melvin Rochester, pulling a laptop from his bag and flipping it open. A video window popped up.

"Hello, Laura." The voice sent an instant chill down Laura's back. Even Christof turned to the screen in recognition. It was Grandad.

"I'm delighted you've got this far. That is to say, I'm not currently delighted, because if you're watching this then I'm dead, which is not delightful news to me, as you'll understand. My capacity for delight will have been severely and permanently curtailed. As I speak, I am delighted, though, or rather, I'm delighted in anticipation of the successful unfolding of my plan - about which I have serious reservations and deep misgivings." He paused. His eyes flicked away from the camera, "This is not going well. I'm going to go out and come back in again." Grandad walked off screen, and then re-entered.

"Hello, Laura," he said again.

"I said at the funeral - or rather I said a couple of minutes ago when I recorded what you saw at the funeral, if that makes sense - that I had been murdered. I was being overly dramatic. There is, I should have said, a 78% chance that I have been murdered. Or rather," his voice changed. Its light edge gone, his eyes sad, "there is a 78% chance that if I had not met Marcus Yolandi, then I would be alive now.

"I will begin with your grandmother. Sylvia Gryene. She is an extraordinary woman. From the moment we met, there was - I cannot now bring myself to call it love - but there was a great respect between us. We conspired to bring your parents together. You were our daughter in a way.

Whilst I spent my life seeking out the bizarre and the mysterious, her genius was in the practical. She knew how to build her business, and she does amazing things, but she has," Grandad struggled for the right word, "she has a flaw. She gets carried away with what she CAN do and she seldom asks if what she is doing is the RIGHT thing."

Grandad coughed, and looked away. He was clearly finding this one-sided conversation difficult. He forced himself to stand and look straight at the camera, "When I became ill," he said, "I was told I had a good chance. I was told there were treatments. I'm not going to go into exactly what they were. But they were hard. The operations I could cope with. They were just pain. Being put under again and again. Waking up with a little less of me left, and a little less of it. I could take that."

Laura watched her Grandad through the screen. She felt as though there was nobody else in the room. Nobody else in the world. She remembered those operations. The family watching as he went under, joking, and woke up always with a line. "They cut off the wrong bit." He had once told her. Another time, he said, "The surgeon left his watch - he has to go back and get it," but each time, they knew what it meant. It meant there was more. More to be cut and scraped out.

The figure on the screen continued, "There came a point where what was left of my tumour was inaccessible to the knife. But they had good news - they had a course of drugs, and if I kept to them. If I saw it through, I could make a full recovery. They couldn't be certain, of course. You'll learn that about doctors. They'll never give you a straight answer. Go in with a bruised knee, and they'll tell you that you

SHOULD make a full recovery," he smiled weakly, "but they'll never tell you that you WILL. 78% was the figure I heard. More than three quarters chance!

"And then they began the drugs," Laura watched as Grandad sank into a chair. He looked suddenly drained at just the thought, "Laura, I cannot tell you what it was like. Dozens of pills every day. Each one a different flavour of poison. Some created nausea. Some blocked it. Some made me sleep when I wasn't tired, others kept me constantly awake when I was. Each one on a schedule that had to be kept to day and night. The routine was the only thing I could fit in my mind. I could feel them, day by day, night by night rotting my body, blurring my mind. Some days I couldn't eat, or drink, or talk or think. I couldn't take it, Laura. I'm not a strong man. I live by laughing off pain. I suppose I'm lucky I got this far in my life before I found something I couldn't laugh away.

Grandad cleared his throat. It sounded hoarse and dry. Laura watched his eyes, unable to look away. "And then one day, your grandmother visited. I begged her for something. Anything that would deliver me from this, and she sent me Marcus Yolandi.

"He was like an angel, Laura," he said. "Where the doctors and nurses rushed in and out, he spent time with me. Where they pumped me with one medicine after another, constantly without explanation, Marcus explained to me exactly what he was going to give me and why. And exactly what it would do. He gave me answers, and I was weak and desperate, and I believed him."

Laura stared. She had known none of this. Grandad had said nothing, and she hadn't asked. She just turned up at the hospital and watched him die.

"The moment I stopped taking what the doctors had given me. The moment I switched to Marcus' pills, I started feeling better. Much better. I could sleep again. I could get out of bed. I could think! Laura, it was a revelation.

"The doctors told me my tumour had shrunk to invisibility, and I was even getting my appetite back. That's when I started to read. I researched the treatment. It seemed like a miracle, and I was so angry that while this simple pill was easily available, my doctors were eviscerating me with twenty chemical poisons a day. That was when I found out what was in these magical pills, and do you know what it was?" Grandad stared out at Laura, his eyes angry, ashamed. She felt her own eyes filling with tears.

"Yes, Grandad." she whispered, "I know."

He answered her, "Of course you do. You're cleverer than I ever was, aren't you? It was nothing. Water. Just water. There was no cure." He coughed again. Harder this time. A dry retching sound.

"By the time I worked it out, it was too late. The real medication couldn't stop it. I was finished. But I still had my mind. And one last idea," Grandad's head was bowed. Suddenly he looked up, determined and strong. He stared straight into the camera. "Revenge," he said simply.

Behind him, a grey cat hopped up onto the table. Its tail wagging slowly from side to side. Christof Tourenski, Grandad's revenge.

The video cut off abruptly. Melvin Rochester spoke now, "Your grandad decided to set up a grand hoax - to show how absurd the whole alternative medicine industry was. To create an entirely fake doctor, complete with meaningless qualifications obtained online, bogus tales of derring do and miracle cures. All of it so absurd and transparent that any fool could see through it, but yet so compelling and convincing that nobody in the whole corrupt alternative marketplace would want to"

"But why?" asked Laura. "What's the punchline?" Grandad always had a punchline.

"Why, you!" said Rochester, "You're the punchline. You and your cat. Dan Pan and I have been running the online life of Christof Tourenski ever since your Grandfather died. Building him up as a great alternative healer with links to all the quack cures under the sun. And on Saturday, there will be a mass rally where every quack therapy and New Age treatment will converge the Houses of Parliament. And the guest speaker will be Christof Tourenski himself. When you stand up there, and reveal that this great guru is just a house-cat, the whole movement will be discredited." Melvin Rochester smiled. It looked like it might break his face.

Laura drummed her fingers on the desk, her head reeling. Even by his standards, Grandad had outdone himself with this one. Christof, oblivious curled himself up on the table.

"Why couldn't you just tell me?" she shouted at Rochester. "Don't I have any say in this plan?"

"That was precisely why your Grandfather forbade us from telling you anything," he said. "You had to work it out for yourself. He said you'd figure it out and you'd find us. Frankly, I was skeptical, but here you are."

"Here I am," she said, "but it didn't go quite as planned, did it? Dan Pan is gone. Marcus Yolandi is trying to kill me. And now the Prince of Wales wants me to advise him on turmeric!"

"Yes," said Rochester, "It does all seem to have got rather out of hand, doesn't it?"

"Is that all you've got to say?" Melvin Rochester put his hands together as though praying. He was quiet for so long that Laura began to suspect that this was indeed all he had to say. Laura glared at him. "Dan Pann is probably dead by now."

"He's not dead," said Rochester, calmly, "at least not yet."

"How can you possibly know?"

Rochester pulled out his mobile. He flicked it on, and a message popped up on the screen, "I received this just before you arrived," he said. He handed her the phone. It was a text from Dr. Dan.

It read, "Find me: 472336"

"I didn't understand what it meant until now," He said, "He must have sent it after he was caught. It's a password for his mobile account. I can use it to track his phone's GPS signal."

He stood up suddenly.

"Go home," he said. "Go home and wait. I'll find out where he is, then, once I know what we're dealing with, I'll get the police in. I may need you tomorrow. Do not let the animal -" he gestured towards Christof -" out of your sight."

"I can't go home. They know where I live," she said.

"You'll be safe as long as you're with your parents," he said. He obviously didn't know her parents, thought Laura, but he was probably right. Yolandi would not want extra witnesses, and whatever was behind Granny Gryene's involvement, Laura couldn't believe she wanted her dead.

Rochester stood and strode towards the door. "We should leave here separately," he said.

"Wait!" said Laura. She had suddenly remembered something. "Tomorrow is the court hearing," But Rochester had gone.

Chapter 15: A Cat in Hell's chance

There was a certain genius to Peter, thought Laura as she sat in the living room that evening, listening to his plan. When he had an idea, it was not like other people's ideas. It was not a natural next step from where you were towards where you wanted to be, or even a clever sidestep to avoid an obstacle. It wasn't even a brave change of direction. When Peter had an idea, it whisked you with dizzying vertigo from wherever you had been and deposited you on a whole new landscape. Frequently one with more dangers and more obstacles than the one you were in to begin with, only with the perception of benefit that came from not immediately being able to see the perils before you.

This particular idea was typically Peter. It was completely out of the blue, it was driven by desperation, and it was far, far too late.

"We're going to transfer the sanctuary to a new owner," he explained, "The NLFPC will have to start their inspections again - we can make changes - we'll have time -we'll make it work!" he insisted.

"But the case is first thing tomorrow morning," said Laura. "Where are you going to find someone stupid enough to take the place on - while it's being sued - and with no way of turning it around?"

Any new owner would have to be a complete idiot. Someone with no concept of the problems facing the sanctuary, and no idea of what they were letting themselves in for. "Even if you could find someone foolish enough to do it, how are you going to get the paperwork signed before the hearing?"

Judy smiled. "The paperwork is all here," she pushed a sheaf of printed documents under Laura's nose. "All you have to do is sign it."

"You have to be joking," she said.

Laura looked back and forth between her parents. They were not joking.

Laura slept deeply and woke with just one focus. She got out of bed and stared at herself in the bedroom mirror. Peter's plan was awful and there was just the slimmest chance of making it work. But, it was all that was left.

Dead Cat Day was coming. The day when she would have to bring out each cat in turn, and submit it to the vet's needle. She had seen it, months, years ahead, and she had failed to stop it, but now the face staring back at her out of the mirror was all there was. This face, standing in front of the judge and making the mess they'd agreed on last night sound like a rescue plan.

She could only hope that Rochester would manage to rescue Dr. Dan while she was in court, and that the ensuing police questions would wait until the hearing was over. Being dragged out of the hearing to answer questions about a kidnapping probably wouldn't help their case.

Slowly, she wiped away the feral creature who had spent the previous night on the stone floor of the cat's home. The strange cat-girl who had pitched up at a garden party and talked with government and royalty with her dark eyeliner and her crazy hair. She had to go. She would be no help today.

Piece by piece, Laura rebuilt herself in the mirror. She had decided on her image for today. Simple makeup. Immaculate hair, tied up. A suit. She judged herself in the mirror, and focused detail by detail, comparing each to the class and the poise of the character she was trying to emulate.

Today, she was going to be, in every possible way, Granny Gryene.

Laura brushed the last of the cat hairs from her suit, left Christof on the bed and stepped out of her room. Her parents were fussing in their bedroom.

"We will go now," she said, simply

"I just feel the need to check the -" started Judy.

"Get in the car. We are leaving now," commanded Laura. Channeling Granny Gryene felt good. If she was going to be put in charge of this disaster, then she would run it her way. Surprisingly, her parents capitulated immediately. Peter straightened his tie, and smoothed his least crumpled corduroy suit. Judy abandoned the pretense of organising the documents in a tatty box file, and they both filed out and followed her down the stairs.

She looked back just once when she got to the door.

"Ready?" she said. They nodded behind her and she threw open the front door.

The world went white.

Slowly, the white faded to the clattering strobe light of dozens of camera flashes. Outside the door, a sea of press were waiting, lenses trained on Laura and her parents. The shouting began - each photographer desperate to attract Laura and her parents' attention - but there were so many, it was impossible to tell what they were asking.

They started to close in. Laura dived forward into the crowd, and her parents followed. She fought her way towards the car, half blinded by the flashes and stumbling through a tangle of arms and legs and bodies, microphones buzzing around her mouth like angry flies.

For a moment she lost her sense of direction. The crowd seemed to be everywhere, pressing inwards around her. She tripped, and stuck her hand out for balance. It struck the back window of the old car, and she wrenched open the door, stumbling in and jamming it closed behind her. Cameras pressed up against the window, cracking against the glass and lighting up the interior like little bolts of lightning.

Judy made it into the front of the car, and they both watched Peter struggle, gangling across the bonnet before finally crashing into the driver's seat, and slamming the door.

"What the hell was that?" said Laura as they finally drove away. Two of the more desperate and fittest members of the press pack were running down the road after them. Laura watched as they slowed to a halt and gave up.

"I put a press release out to the local papers," said Peter "It must have worked!"

Laura looked back. The local papers had about three journalists between them, and if any of them had wanted an interview, they'd have phoned first and expected tea and biscuits. No. This would not be the local papers. One way or another, this would be Christof Tourenski, or Dr. Dan.

The family parked up, and Laura led them in, and they sat outside the courtroom waiting in silence for the proceedings to start. If the local papers had any interest in proceedings, they would have sent a reporter to the court, but there was nobody. Laura and her parents sat on the hard plastic chairs waiting for their turn, and were studiously ignored by everyone who entered or left the building. The anonymity and the silence should have been a relief for

Laura, but somehow it was not. She felt as though there was an axe suspended over her head, and she was waiting for it, and a number of other axes, to begin to rain down on her.

Finally, Peter broke the silence. "Judy and I are so glad you're with us - it means - um - a lot," he mumbled.

Before she could reply, the big doors opened, and Judy and Peter gripped each other's hands as they were led through into the chipboard opulence of the courtroom. It was as though the designers had seen the oak and leather of the parliamentary committee room she had been in the previous afternoon, and tried to reproduce it using flat-pack furniture.

Laura steeled herself. This was it. All or nothing. In her head, she went through what she was going to say. Even with Kennington Paws nominally in her hands now, there was no guarantee that anything would change. She would have to convince them that she, as the new owner had a plan, which she didn't, that the transfer rendered the case void, which she wasn't at all sure about, and that this wasn't all just a ploy to play for time - which it quite definitely and transparently was.

Laura was slightly behind, and as she peered round the door, she could see the NLFPC representative, the angel of death waiting at the other side of the court. He was staring straight ahead, plainly terrified. He was, it seemed, more comfortable issuing summons from his office than he was standing up in court and facing those he accused. He looked a reluctant, weedy little harbinger of doom, and Laura couldn't help feeling sorry for him shaking in the dock, but pitiful or not, this man was about to tear her family apart, and unleash death on eighty animals which, she, had to accept were morally, emotionally, and now legally, her responsibility.

She closed her eyes for a second. This was it.

As she stepped through the door to take her place in the court, a hand caught her arm and dragged her back. It was Melvin Rochester.

"Come on!" He said. "I've located Dr. Dan. We have to go now." Peter turned, looking back at her. She just caught her father's expression of panicked abandonment as the big doors swung closed in front of her. "Now!" insisted Rochester.

"I can't!" protested Laura.

"He will be killed," stated Rochester, "If we don't go right now!"

She looked at the court door, then back at Rochester. "Ok - five minutes, then! Where are we going?"

"Africa."

"I've traced the GPS in Dr. Dan's phone," said Rochester, as he ushered her into his car. It was one of those vehicles in which the dashboard resembled the controls of a starship, and had enough space on top to store a small cow. "From the speed and direction, he's on a private plane on the way to somewhere in Uganda."

"Why?" Said Laura. Rochester jabbed the car into gear, and buried his foot in the carpet. The car, being modern, filled with electronic safety features, and not designed for high-speed getaways, sedately and gently slid away from the curb with barely a sound.

"Our friend Marcus Yolandi has clinics in Uganda. That's where he ships all Gryene's pills to." said Rochester, "I'm guessing that's where he's going. They only set off this morning, so we're just a few hours behind."

"Why take Dr. Dan there?"

"It's a fairly lawless place," said Rochester, "I imagine, in London, holding a hostage is risky - and disposing of a body too. In Uganda, if one knows how the regime works, I imagine one might do anything one pleases."

"And we're going to stop him? How?"

"I have a private jet waiting." Said Rochester.

Laura stared at him, "You don't have a private jet!" she said.

"I've borrowed one," he admitted. "I do a lot of TV work. I've had to pull in a few favours from friends."

"Friends with private jets?" said Laura.

"Put it this way. I've had to agree to Dan and I going on 'I'm a celebrity, get me out of here'. If we survive." He paused. "I'm in two minds about which I would prefer."

"Fine. Why are the press outside my house?" asked Laura.

Rochester thrust a newspaper into her lap. On the front cover was a photo from the garden party. In the foreground, Christof, proud and upright, facing down the two government cats - breaking up, the caption claimed, a long-running feud between the Foreign Office, and the Treasury. In the background, Laura, flanked by the Prince of Wales, and the Minister for Health. Looking on, a crowd of the great and the good from all walks of public life. It made quite an image.

"Tourneski's cat - the mystery peacemaker," the headline underneath screamed. The article indicated that the hunt was now on, for the reclusive healer, his incredible cat, and the mysterious and 'feisty' Laura Shatner, the only person in the world Christof Tourneski entrusted to be his public face. Laura felt physically sick. Everyone she knew would see this. Even mad people would think she was mad now. For the rest of her life, she would be "that mad girl with the cat."

Even Samuel, leafing through the paper in his gun shop would think Laura was some kind of nutter. And even worse would be anyone who thought she was sane. They would think she was on their side. That she believed in whatever crackpot fantasy they were hawking. "Laura Shatner," they would say. "She believes in rebirthing," or "beer spas," or "drinking her own urine."
.
 If the option existed for her to join Christof in his non-existent hermitage she would have taken it instantly, and slipped seamlessly into the realm of fiction.

"It's going far better than we could ever have hoped," Melvin Rochester smiled at her. He obviously didn't see the problem.

"We'll need my passport," said Laura, as they reached the end of her road, "pull in here. We can't be photographed together. The press think we're enemies."

Rochester spun the wheels abruptly towards the pavement. The car hesitated, and then floated gracefully to the kerb, and stopped. She climbed out of the car and made a dash for the door. She managed to take most of the photographers by surprise, and got to the door without too much trouble.

She ran into her room, and grabbed her passport. She was just about to leave when she noticed Christof lying on the bed exactly where she'd left him. She grabbed him too, climbed out of the back window, hopped over the fence, and sprinted through next-door's garden. By the time she hit the road, she had been spotted, and about twenty photographers were after her. They ran, closely packed and flashing like a swarm of overweight fireflies.

Laura hit the side of the car, flung the door open and jumped in. Rochester jammed his foot on the accelerator, and gripped the steering wheel. His car moved off with the gently rising hum of a departing lift.

"You can't take the animal to Africa," said Rochester.

"I can't leave him here," she said. If the press did not get him, anything might happen at the court case now, and things could change very fast.

"Well, what are we going to do?" Said Rochester. There was only one thing for it.

"Stop here!" she said suddenly. Rochester jammed his feet hard on the breaks, and the car slowly idled to a stop outside Samuel's military junkshop.

Laura climbed out, and took Christof in. Samuel was, predictably, reading today's paper. He looked up.

"Is this you? "He started, pointing at the front page.

"I need you to look after my cat," she said, as she dumped Christof onto the counter where she had placed the gun a couple of days earlier. Samuel's reaction was considerably less positive.

"I don't like cats," he said.

"Neither do I," said Laura. It was a reflex response, which she had lately come to realise, did not fit with the evidence, "Feed him twice a day, and don't let anyone see him!" She handed him the lead, "And give me your phone number." He did so without question. She wrote it down, and walked out without another word.

"We could maybe go out - somewhere - maybe?" she heard him gabble behind her. She pretended she hadn't heard, and shut the door behind her.

Laura hopped into the car. "Get us to the airport," she snapped, and Rochester wrenched the steering wheel. The car waited for a gap in the traffic, and then smoothly took them up to 20mph. They headed for the airport.

Chapter 16: Margin of Error at 20,000 Feet

Rochester's borrowed jet was the transport of choice for those who were above petty concerns like money or greenhouse gas emissions. From the outside, it was sleek, but disappointing. It was dwarfed by the passenger jets which passed in the distance on their thunderingly impossible take-offs, and it seemed merely average amongst the huddle of private planes, abandoned without apparent order, on the tarmac of London City Airport.

On the inside, it was something different. Conclusive evidence that money and taste were not just uncomfortable bedfellows, but estranged partners going through a particularly messy divorce.

Wood, overstuffed white leather, gold chrome and plastic fused to form an interior that attempted to convey stylish grace, but in fact gave the impression of a caravan decorated by a pimp.

Rochester made himself instantly at home, and Laura followed, strapping herself into the nearest seat. Almost immediately, the plane began to move. They turned onto the runway, and the plane started to accelerate, pushing her back into her seat. No going back now.

Right now, her parents would be struggling to defend themselves in court. Confused and abandoned, Peter would be bumbling and ranting, Judy would be evading, and transferring every question. Laura could hear her now, telling the prosecution solicitor that she felt his aggression, and inviting him to explore his feelings with the group.

It would get them nowhere. She was the only person who could have helped, and she was 50, 60 100, 1000 feet from the ground, and accelerating. Laura looked out of the window, and tried to make sense of the landmarks of London as they sped away. If she could see the court - place the area as they flew over - but she couldn't. And soon the low, London cloud swallowed everything.

"Do you think he's dead already?" she said.

"I don't know," said Rochester, "his phone is still on. That's all I know," he paused. "There's a chance, at least."

More than the cats had, then, thought Laura.

The plane was, at least, well supplied with complimentary newspapers. A range of them was spread across a gold rimmed glass table in front of her. Her photo stared out from most of them. It was awful.

The news media was pushing two parallel lines of story. The first story was about her as Christof Tourenski's enigmatic envoy and her rise through the celebrities and opinion formers celebrating breakfast on the lawn of the walled garden.

Papers differed on whether it was a craze or a cult, but one way or another, the ubiquitously absent figure of Christof Tourenski was sucking in every New Age fad diet, every questionable herbal remedy, and every bizarre treatment ancient or modern. From Paleolithic diets to DNA therapy administered over the phone, everyone wanted a piece of Christof Tourenski.

It was a virtuous circle. Each therapist that spoke out to back the new guru gained instant respect from their proximity to him, and each in turn lent the hot air of their credibility to inflate Christof further. The fact that Christof himself was absent meant that each observer could take him as their own, form him in their image. He was not there to make misjudged comments, to be cut down by critics, or to prove himself fallible in any way. And without the encumbrance of corporeal existence, his reputation grew and grew.

The whirlwind which Grandad had unleashed had grown to a hurricane, and its growth showed no sign of slowing.

The press' second line of story focused around Christof Tourenski, Laura's cat. Nobody knew the name of the animal yet, but they did know that it was part, somehow, of the Christof Tourenski phenomenon. The cat, having faced down the Treasury and the Foreign Office and settled the territorial dispute between them, was now being heralded as some kind of peacemaker among cats, prompting near hysteria on the subject of the sentience of the feline species.

Christof (the cat) was, by his connection to Christof (the man), being credited with courage, knowledge, and wisdom way beyond his intelligence, his species, and any credible explanation.

The plan, Rochester explained to her as they hurtled over the European continent, was that the moment Laura stood up in front of a rally of a thousand people, at the gates of Parliament, and brought those two lines of story crashing together by revealing that Christof and her cat were one and the same, Grandad's bomb would be detonated. The myth would be punctured, and down would come Christof, bringing with him the whole edifice of alternative medicine. Thereafter, an age of rationalism would dawn across the nation. All would bask in the pursuit of true knowledge and reason, and the world would be a better place.

God, he was arrogant!

"You're so sure you're right, aren't you?" she said to him. "How do you know that there's nothing in any of these medicines?"

He looked up from the tabloid newspaper he was leafing through, scoffing at every page. "We don't," he said simply.

"Then Sylvia Gryene might be right? Marcus Yolandi might be right." she said. "They might have the cure to cancer and you're trying to stop them."

"They might," said Rochester. "Anyone might. The whole discipline of medicine grew out of herbalism and traditional cures." Laura had seen a lot over the past few days. She had met people with ideas that were plainly absurd. She had seen medicines made of poison and pills with, apparently nothing in them. But she had taken them and they had worked on her. She had talked to scientists, and doctors and princes, and even the Minister for Health. She had seen one of her grandparents extolling the virtues of alternative medicine, and the other claiming it had killed him. Nothing made sense anymore.

"So all this is just about your ego? You have to put these people down because they don't fit in with your view of the world."

Rochester closed the newspaper and placed it on the table. "Science doesn't advance by someone having a clever idea about how the world works," he said, slowly. "The breakthrough happens when someone tests their hypothesis against the real world, and finds that it works. If something works, then it doesn't matter if it's made by scientists or by fairies." He jabbed his finger at her. "The point is, you have to test it before you can *know.*"

"Every time someone uses one and it works, that's a test," said Laura. "I used one for food poisoning - it worked!"

"Not good enough," said Rochester.

"Exactly - it's not good enough that it works in real life," said Laura, warming to her theme, "As far as you're concerned it's got to pass some special test you've invented."

"No," he said. "It's easy." He sat forward in his seat. "Take 100 people with food poisoning. Give 50 of them your medicine. Give the other 50 an exactly identical pill with nothing in it." He paused. "The only rule is that nobody - not even the person giving the pill - knows who's getting the real medicine."

"Why not?"

"Because people with food poisoning get better anyway. And if someone gives you a medicine, it makes you feel as though you're supposed to get better, and so often you do."

"That's rubbish," she said, "I've heard of placebos. I'm sure they only work on dumb people."

"They work on everyone," Rochester said. "That feeling that something is being done for you is the most universally successful treatment in the history of medicine." He thought for a minute. "It doesn't cure cancer, though," he said softly.

"You can't tell me that's all there is to it!" she said.

"That's all there is to it," said Rochester. "You see who gets better fastest, and if on average there's a significant difference between those who took the medicine and those who took the fake pill, you've got evidence."

"Ah," she said, triumphantly, "but everyone is different, aren't they? Everyone responds differently. That's the point!"

"It doesn't matter," said Rochester. "You can apply whatever rules you like to how you treat the test participants - you can give them all different things if you want. The only rule is that you have to do an identical fake treatment to the other half of the group. If you can show your treatment makes more people better quicker, or more completely or keeps them fitter for longer, you've got a cure you can prescribe - congratulations, that's real medicine. If you can't, then all your hypotheses don't count for anything because if it isn't better than nothing then it isn't medicine."

Laura stared out of the window, at the sea of clouds below them. Melvin Rochester was infuriating. He had an answer for everything. That was his job. And he couldn't accept that there might be things he couldn't explain. That, she decided was probably his job too. You couldn't explain away Granny Gryene's whole factory, her whole industry, just on the basis that people *thought* they were feeling better... could you?

She felt angry. Furious, even, and the more she thought about it, the angrier she got. They were using her. Rochester, Dr. Dan, Grandad. They were all using her to deliver their agenda and none of them had stopped to think about how this would affect her.

She had been hunted, haunted, hounded and shot at, and now they expected her to publicly pose as something she was not - to be humiliated in front of thousands of people. To become a figure of ridicule - hate even for millions, and worst of all, they had manipulated her into rejecting her grandmother and her parents in the cruelest possible way, and she did not even know why she was doing it.

"I'm not doing it!" she shouted suddenly, "I don't care if this was Grandad's idea. I don't want to be part of it."

"You have to!" said Rochester. "There is too much at stake to back out now!"

"I don't have to do anything!" She balled at him. She stood up and stormed out of the cabin. The only place to go on the small aircraft was the tiny toilet. She slammed the inward opening door as loudly as she could, locked the door and sat on the toilet.

Outside, she could hear Rochester hammering on the door. He just, he said, wanted to talk. Well, Laura did not want to talk. She ignored him, and after about twenty minutes, he finally gave up.

Laura sat on the toilet seething in silence. The tears rolled down her face. Finally, she hauled her phone out of her pocket, and flicked open the spreadsheet app. Her "People I can trust" list was still open. She highlighted Grandpa's name, and deleted it.

She must have fallen into a tearful sleep on the toilet because the feeling of sudden tilting startled her suddenly awake. The plane was turning sharply. She shook her head, unbolted the lavatory door, and headed for the cabin. Rochester was standing at the cockpit door.

"We're turning, "she said.

"I've been tracking the phone," said Rochester. "Are you OK?"

"What do you care?" she snapped.

Rochester seemed about to argue, but he didn't. Instead, he said, "They've landed, so I know where they're heading. Yolandi's website says he has a clinic in this village." He pointed to his tablet. On it was a satellite picture of what appeared to be a couple of yellow roads against a wilderness speckled with brown and occasional green dots. "It's out in the country, so we still have time to catch them. Our pilot has a few local contacts. He says he can get us to an airfield a little closer."

Suddenly something caught Laura's eye over his shoulder. A large TV hung between two faux marble pillars at one end of the cabin. The sound was down, but images from the news flickered across it. Amongst them, Laura saw a face she recognised. There was a control on the table. She grabbed it, and hit the volume button.

It was Ms. Blythe, in full robes with dripping jewelry. Being interviewed about the place of the cat in society. She was as wide-eyed and mystic as ever.

"Oh, yes," she was saying, "It's a well-known fact that the sound of a cat's purr can cure broken bones."

"Oh, God!" sighed Rochester.

Ms. Blythe was on form. She had, she said, met Laura and her cat before, and although she didn't know Christof's name, she had sensed his deep spirituality. She described, as though it were a proven fact, the way in which our loved ones returned to us in the form of cats, and cited evidence from the Egyptians, from Mesopotamia, and even mentioned the gods of the Vikings. She had been listening to Peter's lectures even if Laura hadn't.

As the camera panned out, it became clear that she was not alone. Ms. Blythe had set up some kind of vigil, at the doors of the walled garden. Food had been placed simultaneously in two bowls to symbolise, she told the audience, the new-found friendship across the political divide, although currently neither cat was partaking in the offering. Behind her, a crowd of cat people was gathered. Strange and disconnected, they hovered behind her like aliens dressed in human skins.

This wave of publicity around Christof's intervention was Ms. Blythe's moment, and she was seizing it with both hands. In the background, passers-by were stopping, curious at the ritual. Most glanced, and then walked briskly on. A few, the more particular souls, paused, craned their necks. Huddled in towards the speaker.

The Cat People were on the move.

Chapter 17: The road to Hell

The airport's rugged runway had probably never seen an aircraft like theirs before. It certainly felt as though the plane was not keen to set down as it bumped to a halt on the rough tarmac. The crop sprayers and local vegetable transport planes lined up in the fields beside the runway looked as though they could have been there for decades.

"We're not strictly supposed to land here," said Rochester reassuringly, "but don't worry, neither are most of the visitors."

"Great," said Laura, not reassured.

The pilot called Rochester over and gave him a few instructions. Rochester and Laura stepped out into the hot dusk, and made their way, unguided to a tin building which would have served any other airport very well as a tool shed. Here, it was the terminal building, but it was still decorated inside very much as a tool shed would be.

A chubby man rushed over, the moment he saw them, Rochester held his hand out in stiff, British handshake. It was brushed aside, and the man hugged him like an old friend.

"Our pilot tells me you've got a car for us," said Rochester.

"Of course, "said the man, his voice was so deep and full that Laura thought his entire ample body must have been hollowed out to contain nothing but a resonating chamber. "It is my car. You must take my car!"

"Are you sure?" said Rochester.

"Of course, of course!" said the man. He led them over to a car parked just outside under a tall lamp. It was a vehicle of two halves. The top, white. Clean, polished even. The bottom, an indistinguishable texture of rust and red mud. The car had clearly already served its proud master far longer than its manufacturers had ever imagined that it should.

The man held out the keys, and Rochester went to take them. The man closed his other hand over Rochester's, and held it tight. "2,000 US dollars" he said in the same, deep charming tone, his face not losing one atom of its genial generosity.

Rochester fumbled in his pocket, and handed over a wad of notes.

Neither the car, nor the rough dirt road, were prepared to be as forgiving to Rochester's driving style as their counterparts in England. The moment he touched the accelerator, the wheels spun into the dust and the car skated sideways. He yanked the wheel to correct the spin, and the back wheels immediately lost all grip, throwing them around in a dizzying spiral. Laura gripped the dashboard, and shut her eyes, but Rochester did not seem to have taken his foot off the accelerator. Instead, he steered wildly, trying to bring the vehicle back under control. As they straightened, Laura opened her eyes again. They were heading straight for the flimsy fence around the airfield.

Hitting it would do the car little damage. However, just on the other side of it was parked an aircraft which represented not just a lethal obstacle, but also several million pounds worth of borrowed engineering, and their only way out of the continent of Africa.

Laura turned to Rochester. He had given up on the steering wheel entirely, and resigned himself to the impact, shielding his face with his arms. Laura felt a respected scientist might have made a more considered calculation involving the weight of the plane versus the strength of his arms, and the potential benefits of taking his foot off the gas. However, there it was.

She leant over, grabbed the wheel, and at the same time, lifted her foot over the gear stick, and jammed it down on the car's middle pedal.

The vehicle swerved, skidding, grazed itself along the side of the fence for several metres and came to a stop.

Laura leaped out, and dragged Rochester out of the car by his shirt.

"I'm driving!" she yelled at him, and plonked herself into the driving seat. Reluctantly, Rochester climbed in next to her.

"I didn't know you could drive," he said sheepishly.

"I can't!" spat Laura, and the car juddered, and lurched away down the road, "Which way?"

There was only one road away from the airfield, and Rochester pointed down it. He pulled out his phone and the blue light from its screen lit his face in the growing darkness. "They're a couple of hours ahead. It's this direction, but the mobile signal is patchy."

The settlement they were driving through was little more than a support structure for the airfield. The activity of flying out crops had created a buzz of habitation, a few warehouse buildings. The odd shop. But the sharp-edged flat pack buildings in machine cut wood and metal were thinning out already, being replaced by less precise dwellings, leaning together for support. Corrugated tin roofs, walls in mismatched brick, wood or dirt, and sometimes all three in patchwork, were replacing them, and even these started to become less crowded after a few minutes of driving.

"What's the time in England?" Laura said suddenly.

"About 8 pm,"

Laura gasped, grabbed her phone from her pocket, and flicked it on.

"You shouldn't do that while you're driving." Said Rochester, sulkily. Laura glared at him, and hit speed-dial. A distant voice answered. It was Judy. Laura could barely hear her over the sound of the car.

"Where are you?" said Judy. She sounded flat. Defeated.

"What happened in court?" asked Laura. The sound that came out of the phone was just sobbing.

Eventually, Judy managed, "Why did you go?"

"I had to." said Laura, feeling the tears behind her eyes.

"Why?" pleaded Judy. Laura swallowed hard. That conversation was going to be a long and difficult one, and the faltering phone signal would not support its weight. Judy was cutting out already.

"Hang on," Laura said, desperately over the breaking line. "Just keep them off until I get back. I've got a plan." The phone crackled and faded. The line was dead.

"We need you!" was the last thing Laura heard.

"Have you really got a plan?" Rochester asked after a long silence.

"Shut up," she said. "Just shut up." There was no plan. Maybe there was an idea in her head. A seed of something - not even half a plan. Perhaps she had just needed to say it.

Eventually, the buildings dwindled to nothing, and the night became properly dark. Rochester fell asleep beside her, but it didn't matter. There were no turnings, and no variation in the road. It ran straight through the flat countryside. Occasionally a scattering of wooden or rusting tin sheds which could have been houses would emerge in the headlights. Beside them, piles of wood, red and blue crates, and the occasional bicycle, and away from the road, roughly cultivated fields were grouped, separated by lines of scraped up earth.

The settlements appeared up ahead, and were passed in seconds, receding into the dark, leaving Laura following a road barely distinguishable from the scrubland to either side. Several times, she veered off the road, alerted only by the change in texture of the ground beneath the wheels, or a sudden tree up ahead. She swerved back onto the track, and carried on. Outside of the headlights' range, she could see nothing but a rich horizon of stars. Every so often, two stars would detach, grow, and turn into another pair of headlights passing, and going on into the dark behind.

She felt the car was tiny. A bubble of tangible reality in a mad, dangerous world. Fleeing away from home, and its unfolding horrors of unwanted fame and cat slaughter which she could not now stop, and towards a GPS dot flashing on a mobile screen, and another horror which she could not understand, but somehow knew would be infinitely greater.

Chapter 18: The Miracle

Dawn broke in silence, and then exploded in the most glorious and joyous traffic jam Laura had ever experienced.

At one moment, the road was empty and quiet, and then they peaked a hill and suddenly they were in amongst it. Cars, minibuses, lorries, and coaches, each one crowded with laughing people, and each decorated with tree branches, flowers, and shreds of multi-coloured plastic and paper jostled along the road.

From within came the sounds of shouting, cheering and singing. It was an atmosphere like that of a football stadium or a carnival. Laura joined the throng, and next to her, Melvin Rochester stirred into life. From the vehicles around them, faces beamed. Thin faces, tired faces. Some desperately so, but all laughing, singing, shouting, waving flags and branches, they urged their drivers forward as though their voices were fuel.

Looking around, Laura and Rochester were instantly caught up in it, smiling back despite themselves. Despite their tiredness. Despite the road, and the worry, and the vehicles around them, swerving like insane dodgems. This was no ordinary queue of traffic.

Instead of waiting patiently, one behind the other along one side of the narrow dirt road, the vehicles here travelled in parallel. They spilled out sideways from the road on both sides, turning a single lane road into a multi-lane motorway.

The traffic was slowed by everyone's general aim to be, at some point, on the actual original road, and their vague desire to avoid trees, and each other in so far as was practical. However, pace was still brisk, and good natured competition kept them from slowing too much.

Laura grinned out of the window, as they jostled past a pickup truck. Sitting in the back of it, a group of young men waved, their faces split by huge laughing smiles. Between them, another man was propped, his head bobbing, and lolling as they bumped along the road. He looked weak, but managed a smile as his eyes connected with Laura's. The man shakily raised one finger, pointing along the road towards their unseen destination, and then let the hand drop into his lap. His companions cheered.

Laura looked over at Rochester and laughed, caught up in the mysterious joy of the procession.

Rochester was staring at the man. Suddenly a look of shocked realisation spread across his face. He raised both hands to his mouth. His eyes widened in horror.

"No!" he gasped. "No, he can't be!"

"What?" said Laura.

"Get us through!" he said. "You have to get us to the front!" Laura stared at him, "Now!" he shouted.

She gunned the car, and took it between two buses and out to the side of the road, where there was less traffic. She hit the accelerator hard, and they bumped over tufts of rough grass and rocks, picking up speed. She went wider around the other outliers. In the rare instants when the front wheels crashed into the ground, she jerked the steering wheel to bounce them around the larger shrubs and the few off-road vehicles that had come out so far away from the road.

Melvin Rochester's face had gone grey, and he was shaking his head as though he had seen something so shocking he could not believe or accept it.

Laura pressed on, passing the jostling cars on the outside. The terrain was rough, and the little car rocked and crashed. They hit a rock, and the bumper flew off, but they didn't stop, and soon they were close to the front of the procession. Up ahead, there were buildings. Rough, temporary huts patched together out of thrown-away building materials. They were densely packed and seemed to be arranged without design or thought.

It reminded Laura of something. A refugee camp, perhaps? Rochester told her to park, and they continued into the town on foot.

"What is it?" said Laura eventually, as they picked their way between strangely silent crowds of dwellings. Rochester didn't answer. He just kept walking straight ahead towards the centre of town.

As they passed a doorway, Laura peered in. The sun was bright now, and the inside darkly shadowed so that she could barely see. A woman lay on the floor, covered in a blanket. She moved slowly as she turned to look out, as though her head were a heavy, dead weight.

On the floor beside her, two children played silently and without joy.

Laura turned and walked on after Rochester. Up ahead, he had stopped where the patched up shacks ended abruptly at an open dust road. He was staring at something just out of her view.

She approached and stood beside him. The buildings of the clinic were a stark contrast to the shacks hashed together in a growing town around them. They were bright, shining white in the sunlight, brand new, and clean, and around them, a tall, wire fence, higher than two men, and topped with spirals of razor wire. To the front, a concrete floored compound and two tall, solid gates, and in front of that, the cavalcade of vehicles they had met on the road was starting to arrive, and disgorge its passengers like offerings before the gates.

The crowd was growing all the time. Some walking. Some being helped by friends. Some laughing, some singing. Some being carried. Men and women pressed against the gates.

Laura stopped a woman as she climbed off a rusting bus. She looked old. No. She looked young, but with an old skin and eyes.

"What's happening here?" said Laura. The woman looked at her sideways as though she didn't understand.

Eventually, she said, in English, "The doctor. The doctor - he is here!" The woman leaned close towards her. Her skull was utterly visible, emphasised as though her face was wrapped in cling film, not skin. "He has the cure," she whispered.

"The cure to what?" said Laura. The woman gaped at her as though the question was absurd. As though there was only one illness in the world.

"AIDS," she said.

Laura's head swam. In her mind, her focus shifted from this one woman, outwards. Out to the shining clinic. Out to the crowds pressing around its gates. Out to the town thrown up and growing around it, every shack incubating a dying man or woman. Out to the road, thronged with joyful, hopeful people, at the edge of death and yet flooding in ready to pay their last penny to anyone who claimed they could help.

She felt sick. Grandad had not known the half of it.

Suddenly, the woman's face brightened. She pushed past Laura and struggled towards the gates. At that moment, a cheer went up, and the crowd surged forward.

Inside the gates, on a raised stage, Marcus Yolandi had emerged. He was smiling broadly, his hands raised like a benevolent god. The crowd cheered, and then quietened. He waited for quiet, and then proclaimed to the gathered crowd; "I have returned from England. I have the drugs, and for that we thank this woman!"

He gestured behind him, and Sylvia Gryene stepped out onto the podium. At first, she looked uncertain, nervous, but as her eyes scanned the sea of joyful, hopeful faces, she smiled. She raised her hand to wave, and the crowd roared again. Laura watched her grandmother's face, trying to read her expression.

Yolandi stepped forward again, and gestured for quiet. He paused until every sound had dropped to nothing, then he boomed, "Selection begins today!" The entire crowd erupted. Cheering, chanting, singing broke out. Someone started to beat out a rhythm on the side of a bus door, and more drummers and voices joined in. Within a minute, the sick and dying were dancing in the street as though a party could banish their disease.

Through the crowd she glimpsed Marcus Yolandi's watching, smiling face. The man who had killed her grandfather, tried to kill her - a hero - a god.

Suddenly, it was too much. Laura leaped forward towards the fence. Rochester grabbed her and pulled her back. She fought him, screaming at him to let her go. She batted at him with her fists, but he held on until she slowly calmed.

"You can't get in," he said. He held her wrists and gestured at the crowds by the gate. "They can't get in! Do you think you're more desperate than they are?"

"We have to get Dr. Dan!" she said, "We have to stop this!"

"What are you going to do?" he said. Laura snatched her hands away from his, and stared at him. He was right, of course. They had to have a plan.

Laura and Rochester scouted around the edge of the compound. The tall wire fence went all the way around without a break. At the back, as if to taunt them, a row of bins was sitting outside one of the buildings. Leant against one of them, a row of tools which Laura assumed were used to erect the fencing. One of them was a set of bolt-cutters. They would have made short work of the outer perimeter if they hadn't been stored safely inside the wire fence.

"Maybe we can use them to get out?" said Laura. Rochester shrugged.

By the time they got back to the front, the atmosphere had changed. Marcus, Granny Gryene and a group of big men had come outside the main gates, and begun to set up a series of tables. With them, they had boxes of papers, and a plastic bag full of white jackets. While Marcus handed out papers and white coats to the men, he seemed to be explaining to Granny Gryene the details of what was happening.

The now white-coated and official-looking men organised the piles of papers behind the desks, and a chaotic crowd jostled in front of them to be first to give their names and details.

The crowd pressed forward, as the uniformed men tried to write notes, and passed the sick back and forth between themselves. It appeared that each potential patient had to first give their details, and hand over a large wad of money to one nurse before being passed on to another, and possibly a third. If they managed to negotiate this chaos amongst a hundred or so more or less incapacitated and desperate patients, being hounded this way and that, they were eventually herded into groups and lead through the gates into the compound where they were left to mill around waiting for the next layer in their induction process to begin.

Laura and Rochester were in no danger of being spotted by Granny Gryene or Marcus. The chaos was barely being contained, and even Marcus himself seemed surprised by the number of people thrusting themselves at his gates.

"We'll soon be spotted if we try to get in," observed Rochester, but Laura wasn't listening. She ducked away from his side, and, keeping low, she weaved her way into the crowd. What she was looking for was right under Marcus' nose. She pushed her way through thin legs towards the front of the crowd. There it was, on the ground just out of reach. She looked up. Marcus was pacing, back and forth, dangerously close to her, his eyes darting around the throng trying to keep control of everything.

She froze. Suddenly a voice from the crowd caught Marcus' attention. Someone was arguing with one of his officials, waving a paper in the air. Marcus strode over to him, hands outstretched.

Laura took her chance. She pushed out from between the throng, grabbed the black bag from the ground, and dived back in amongst them, dodging through until she emerged next to Rochester in the shadow of a shack at the other side of the road.

She thrust the bag into his hands.

"What's this?" he said.

"White coats," said Laura. "Something Dr. Dan taught me."

Chapter 19: Kill or Cure

In the end, getting in was easy. The right combination of looking as though they were not there, and looking as though they were supposed to be there meant that when they joined the next party of patients to be ushered through the gates, they were guided in by a nurse who instantly assumed that Laura and Rochester were part of their team. The clinic's staff were used to desperate sick people trying to gain entry to the clinic. Healthy European faces were so unexpected there that they were automatically trusted.

Once inside, patients were left to wander in the courtyard. Most of the staff were busy supervising the selection process outside, and Laura and Rochester quickly found their way into the main building.

There was no leather seated waiting room here. No relaxing indoor water features. No table strewn with inspirational books. Just a security kiosk, now empty, Inside it, a table on which a newspaper sat next to a can of coke and a box of handgun bullets.

To the left and right, corridors lead off into the building. There were no signs. Laura looked questioningly at Rochester. He shrugged back. Laura nodded to the left.

"This way, then," she said.

She headed for the corridor. Rochester hesitated, and then followed. She pushed open a set of double doors, and stepped into a large, dark ward. It was filled with a thick, heavy silence, so powerful and oppressive that it pinned her to the spot, afraid to move.

Eight or ten white metal beds were arranged in rows down either side of the room, and at the far end, the blue white light of a computer screen glowed.

Laura focused on the screen. Her mind forbade her eyes from looking directly at the occupants of the beds, but she could think of nothing else. Her vision became peripheral. The square of screen light at the centre of her sight was a vacuum. A blind spot. All that mattered was the paper thin, mostly still, mostly silent shapes shrouded at the edges of her perception.

She was aware of eyes, wide and white, but sunken. The shapes of heads, bald and round. Elbows sharp like sticks. Lips, dry. She could not look.

Rochester stepped past her to the foot of the first bed. Perhaps the room did not fill him with the same dread as it did her. Perhaps he could focus only on the data - the clipboards attached to the end of each bed. Perhaps had simply seen enough rooms filled with the dying to know how to behave here.

"These people are all dying of AIDS?" whispered Laura after a long silence.

"No." said Rochester, "They all have full blown AIDS," he glanced down at the papers beside the foot of one bed. "But they're dying from different complications. This man has toxoplasmosis - it's a parasite found in cats - harmless to healthy people, but in his case," he shook his head, reading from the notes, "abscesses on the brain, coma." He looked at the man lying still in the bed. "Not long now," he said. He moved on to the next bed, and picked up the next set of notes. "This one, blindness," he checked another, "Fungal Meningitis- could be treated, but -" he trailed off.

Suddenly the woman in the bed on the other side of the room was pushing back her covers. Laura tried not to look at her. She stood, shakily and shuffled towards Laura and Rochester.

Laura held her breath and finally faced her. Her eyes were sticky, and she struggled to open them.

"I have come to a decision, Nurse," she said, "I am leaving now." She pressed a handful of green pills weakly into Laura's hand, and shifted slowly towards the door. "Give them to someone else."

"Stop," said Laura, her voice thin. "You're too ill to go anywhere,"

The woman turned at the door, and looked back, "I came here with my children," she said, "I was accepted onto the programme. They were not. If I live, and they die, then I am wicked, yes?" She didn't wait for an answer, but turned slowly away and shuffled out of the room. "I will die with my family," she said as she shuffled away.

Laura started after her. Rochester touched her arm.

"Leave her," he said. He gestured to her handful of pills, "We both know what these are." Laura looked at the pills. Gryene's of course, but there was something else. Her inaction, suddenly broken, she rushed to the first bedside in the long room, then to the next, and the next.

"Why have they all got the same medication? - If they've all got different symptoms, why is every patient getting the same pills?" she said.

Rochester shrugged, "Who knows with these quacks? Does it matter?" he said.

"You don't understand," said Laura, "Homeopaths believe everyone is different - everybody needs different treatments."

"So?" said Rochester, making his way to the end of the ward where the computer glowed.

"So it doesn't make sense giving everyone the same pills - even if they believed what they were doing themselves," she said.

Rochester ignored her. He picked up a document from a pile next to the screen, and jabbed a finger into the computer keyboard, comparing the on-screen results with the paper. "This is odd," he said. He looked around, "this doesn't feel like a hospital. More like -"

"What?" said Laura.

"I don't know," he said, "They're cataloguing everything," he looked at the screen. "Every treatment, every symptom. It's all being done quite"- he hesitated- "rigorously."

"Meaning?" said Laura.

"Meaning their record keeping is considerably better than their treatment regime. There's something else going on here."

Laura heard a sudden noise outside. The sound of people shouting. She stuck her head through the door. The corridor's window looked out on the main courtyard. The white coated staff had finished their intake of new souls, and were packing up, retreating inside the compound. The rejected sufferers still outside were pushing forward, arms raised, and the staff formed a wall to prevent them getting through. It could have been a scene from a zombie movie. Inside the fence, Yolandi and Granny Gryene were walking quickly back to the main building.

"Come on!" said Laura, "We have to go now! We have to find him!"

She pulled Rochester through the door and into another ward, and then another. Deeper into the building, through room after room crowded with rows of beds. As they went deeper, the inmates became weaker, thinner, slower. Each room was darker than the last, and quieter, and in each, Laura felt the sense of crawling dread grow.

Suddenly, Rochester stopped dead. A side door lead off the ward. Above it, a single red light in a wire cage warned against entry. "Isolation ward!" said Rochester.

"We don't go in, do we?" said Laura, apprehensively.

"Well, the light says we shouldn't," said Rochester. "Could be anything in there. But -"

"But if you were keeping a prisoner, and you didn't want anyone to find them," finished Laura.

Rochester raised a hand to the door, then paused. He held his breath, unable to quite make himself push the door. Laura stepped forward, and put her palm against the wood. She pushed hard and the door swung open. They both stepped through together.

Inside, a curtain of transparent plastic showed a single figure motionless on the bed. The thick plastic sheeting was wrinkled, creased. It blurred and distorted the figure so that Laura could not see the face. On the walls all around, ominous plastic suits and masks were hung up. Breathing apparatus, drips, monitors stood waiting in the corners as though for a command to spring into animated robot life. This was serious stuff.

Laura reached out, grabbed the curtain, and yanked it back.

Chapter 20: Double Blind

Dr. Dan Pan's eyes flicked open, and he struggled momentarily against the bonds that held him to the bed. Laura tore the cloth which had been used to gag him away from his mouth. He gasped for a moment.

"What are you doing here?" he said. "And, actually, where is here?"

"Uganda," said Rochester, tearing away the tape that held him down. Dr. Dan sat up, rubbing his wrists.

"We're here to rescue you," explained Laura. Dr. Dan did not seem as reassured as her comment was intended to make him.

"What did you think you were doing?" said Rochester, angrily.

"I was just looking after Christof," said Dr. Dan, "but once I saw the gun, I knew Yolandi must have more invested in all this than we thought. Something's going on."

"And what is that?" demanded Rochester, "Since you didn't even know what country you were in, I am going to guess you can't tell us!"

"He tied me up in his van at the factory," said Dr. Dan. "He kept asking what we were planning." Dr. Dan shook his head, "I managed to get the text out to you - after that I'm afraid it all got a bit chloroformy. Woke up here."

"Did you tell him anything?" said Rochester.

"Not until we got here - I had to in the end - he threatened to kill me," said Dr. Dan grimly. He nodded at the table next to the bed. On it was a syringe filled with dark liquid. "Poison," he explained. "He wants to start selling all over the world. This clinic is all about building credibility for him somehow - he'll do anything to stop us getting to the rally."

"You're an idiot!" shouted Rochester.

Dr. Dan stood up and looked him straight in the eye. "What did you expect me to do? If we'd done this your way she would be dead!"

"The cat would be dead," said Rochester. "That's all!"

"The cat is the whole point! The cat is what will make this go viral!"

"Viral?" said Rochester.

Dr. Dan stared at him "Without the cat it's just a bunch of scientists debating. You never did understand the need for spectacle, Rochester. That's why your TV programmes are so dull!"

"We could have got another cat," hissed Rochester.

"Do you think we could chat about pets somewhere we're not likely to be murdered?" said Laura, pushing open the door into the ward, "There's a set of bolt cutters by the back fence. That's our way out. Let's go."

She led them out into the dark, silent ward. The moment he saw the rows of beds, and their motionless occupants, Dr. Dan stopped cold, and stared around him. "What is this place?" he whispered.

"Welcome to the clinic," said Rochester. "Don't worry," he added darkly, "they're all being cured with sugar pills." Dr. Dan leapt over to the nearest computer terminal, and clicked it on, scanning through screen after screen.

"Come on," Laura said, "We have to go!"

"They're very thorough with their record keeping, aren't they?" said Dr. Dan.

"I noticed," said Rochester. "They're gathering data. Viral load tests. You can see how much HIV DNA there is in each patient's bloodstream. Graphs showing how it's rising. The infection's story for each person."

"A bit of a waste of time if this is just about flogging pills isn't it?" Dr. Dan grabbed a pile of papers from the desk, and looked suddenly puzzled. "These aren't all the same medication. They look identical, but look here." He pointed to the page. Rochester snatched the paper from him.

"This is a placebo-controlled study!" he said.

Laura looked at the two scientists. "He's going to find us any second! Can we argue about this later?"

"You don't understand," said Dr. Dan. "It *is* about credibility - this isn't just a clinic - it's a set of clinical trials. They're running a series of tests to compare the effect of this homeopathic nonsense against a placebo - and as far as it goes, they are well-run trials - they've got cross-checked records - a complete paper trail to show there's no faking and video evidence. It's all by the book -"

"It's completely unethical!" protested Rochester. "He's persuaded these people to give up on real treatments that work by telling them he's got an outright cure, and then he's giving them nothing!"

"Yes," said Dr. Dan, "but why? Every time anyone does a proper test on homeopathy it comes up with nothing. He's testing a placebo against a placebo - and he must know that by now."

Rochester spun round. "He does," he said. "That's why he's doing it." Dr. Dan looked at him. "Normally we'd test the treatment against the best treatments we have - against anteretrovirals, right? Because against a treatment that works, Gryenes' pills would never win out."

"So?" said Dr. Dan.

"But against a placebo - "

"It would still do nothing," said Dr. Dan.

"But there are shades of 'nothing'," persisted Rochester. "The law of averages says some people would do better than others. Some would live longer just by chance, and if those people were all in the same group..."

Laura peered around the door into the corridor. Any second, Marcus Yolandi and Sylvia Gryene would come looking for their prisoner. "Fine!" she said. "So what?"

Rochester continued. "It's like throwing a dice. The chances I'll get a six are one in six, right?"

"Yes," said Laura.

"But what if I throw sixty dice?" said Rochester.

"You get a six one time in six - you get ten sixes," said Laura.

"Yes, but not every time. Sometimes you get eight sixes, sometimes you get twelve!" said Rochester. "If you keep on throwing those sixty dice, over and over again, then somewhere along the line you'll get a really weird result - repeat it enough and you might get twenty sixes."

"So?" said Laura.

"So then, you just publish that go, and it looks like you've got magic dice," said Rochester, "and you don't mention all the other times you threw your dice."

Dr. Dan was pacing the room. "But to get a statistically significant result he'd have to run the trial over and over - hundreds of groups of victims - tens of thousands of people - just to get one trial that appears to show his pills have an effect!"

Rochester pointed to the computer screen. "He is," he said. "Each ward is its own trial. They bring in a bunch of people, do a blood test to measure the change in viral load. By the looks of this they've been taking new intakes for months."

Laura stared at him. "But what about all the other tests - the ones where everyone just dies?"

"He just junks them," said Dr. Dan. "Bins the results and moves on until, one day, by chance he finds a bunch of people who deteriorate more slowly than average. Once he finds that he can go public claiming he's got a drug that works."

Rochester looked suddenly puzzled. "But that wouldn't be enough to convince the scientific community - they'd want tests they could repeat," he said.

"He doesn't need to convince science," said Dr. Dan, "Science doesn't buy the drugs - governments do. He's just got to sow enough doubt to get into the papers, and then the public starts demanding action and politicians like Geraldine Hartley will buy into it. Scientists can argue that it's nonsense, but then scientists always argue. It's what we do. By the time it all unravels, Yolandi will have cleaned up."

Laura shook her head, "No, my Granny wouldn't do that," she said, quietly, suddenly aware she was talking like a child.

"I'm afraid the evidence does not support that conclusion," said Rochester. Laura was shaking.

Suddenly, she heard voices to her left, and turned to look down the corridor. "Run!" she hissed at Rochester and Dr. Dan. The two scientists looked at each other, and then dived through the door at the other end of the ward. Dr. Dan paused and looked back, but Laura shook her head at him. It was too late for her. She took a deep breath, and turned to face Marcus and Sylvia Gryene, who were approaching down the corridor.

"Mr. Yolandi, and Granny," she said, smiling broadly. "How lovely to see you!"

The two stopped dead, and stared at her.

"Laura?" said Granny Gryene. "What the hell are you doing here?" Her mouth was hanging open. Laura smiled. She could see Marcus' mind racing, and then a sudden realisation. His eyes narrowed, and he launched himself forward at her.

Laura turned and dived back into the ward. Dr. Dan and Rochester had run through the door at the back, and, as far as she knew, they hadn't been spotted. She had to give them time to get away. She looked frantically around. Only one other exit. She paused for a second to allow Yolandi to come crashing through the main door with Gryene just behind him, and spot her, and then she threw herself back into the isolation ward, fighting through the plastic curtain to the back of the room.

Isolation rooms, it instantly occurred to her, rarely had a back door. She spun around to face her pursuers, and, as they barged into the room, she smiled triumphantly at them.

"Too late," she said brightly. "He's gone!"

Marcus flew across the room, grabbing her by the neck. "Where is he? Who's helping you?" he shouted into her face. Laura couldn't answer. His hand was painful around her throat, bruising the skin. She gasped for breath, and raised her hands to try to pull him away, but he was too strong. His hand gripped tighter.

He leaned in towards her. She could smell his breath, dry and strong.

"I thought I was going to have to come back to London," he said. "Thank you for saving me a trip."

Granny Gryene was behind him. "Stop! Stop!" she was saying. He ignored her.

"This could have been so much easier. If I'd killed the cat, I could have let you live. Only one of you had to die. But thanks to your friend, it now has to be you." He had loosened his grip a little, but Laura still couldn't prise his hands away.

"You can't hurt her!" Granny Gryene protested, grabbing his arm.

"I can do anything!" he shouted at her. She stepped backwards. "It's too late for you to start being squeamish now," he bellowed. Then, more quietly, he said. "You have to decide which side you're on."

Granny Gryene swallowed. Her face was pale. Her eyes, sad. The tough businesswoman's mask she wore at work had slipped away, and beneath, Laura's granny stood, suddenly wondering, Laura thought, how all her well-meaning cleverness had led her to this hopeless death filled place.

Laura had never seen her look so old. So damaged. She looked from Laura to the enraged face of Marcus Yolandi.

"Granny, please!" Laura protested.

Slowly Granny Gryene's gaze hardened. Laura could see the mask rebuilding itself in front of her eyes. Her body straightened. Her jaw set solid. Her head lifted. She stepped forward.

"What are you doing?" choked Laura.

Sylvia Gryene leaned over to the table at the side of the bed. On it, the syringe of dark poison was laid out ready for Dr. Dan. She picked it up, paused, and then slowly turned to Yolandi. She raised her arm. For a moment it looked as though she might be about to stab him with it. But no. She turned the needle in her hand, and, and presented it to him.

"Do it," she whispered. "Do it now."

Marcus let go of Laura's neck, and instantly grabbed her arm. Before she could even move, he yanked her forward, and jabbed the needle into her arm. It stung and then burned. He pulled it out again, now only half full, and she staggered backwards, her other hand scrabbling at her arm. Dark poison and dark blood running down through her fingers.

It had all happened in an instant, and in the silence that followed, she stared from her arm to Marcus Yolandi's face, his lips curling into a triumphant smile, to Granny Gryene's face, blank and emotionless.

Suddenly, behind them, the door exploded inwards. Dr. Dan and Rochester were one second too late. Dr. Dan charged at Marcus, knocking the syringe from his hand, but Marcus tossed his thin frame easily aside, spinning him into the shelving at the side of the room. Boxes of medication rained down. Laura's head began to spin.

Rochester reached up, and grabbed the plastic curtain, hanging around the bed. He wrenched it from its rail, and threw it at Marcus as he spun back to face him. The curtain covered him for a second, his arms grappling with it. Dr. Dan grabbed one side, and wrapped it around him, and he flailed wildly. Behind him, Granny Gryene shrank back. She did nothing.

For a second, Rochester, Dr. Dan and Marcus batted at each other with open arms. Two plainly inept fighters against one powerful killer wrapped and blinded by a plastic sheet. Laura felt her vision blurring, detaching her from the events around her. She fought against it.

Marcus was scrabbling at the plastic, trying to unravel himself. He stepped backwards towards where Laura was gripping the wall for support. Through the spinning haze, she saw him begin to free himself. As he stepped, she stuck her foot out behind him. He trod on her leg, half spun, staggered, and toppled back, crashing to the floor. His head hit the wall on the way down.

He shook it, and started groggily trying to get up. Dr. Dan stepped over him, grabbed Laura, and he and Rochester wrestled her from the room.

Chapter 21: Running Out

"Shouldn't have come back for me!" Laura managed, as she half ran, half stumbled between the two men through the ward and out into the corridor.

"You shouldn't have come for me either," said Dr. Dan.

"Could we all just forget about what we should have done and get out of here?" Rochester said.

"You don't understand." Laura lifted up her arm. It felt strange, heavy. There was a smudge of blood and poison, and at its centre, the tiny dark red dot of the needle mark. Dr. Dan stared, horrified.

"He injected you?" he said.

"Yes"

"We'll deal with that later," said Rochester looking back down the corridor. "Can you run?"

"I have to, don't I?" said Laura. A plastic curtain and a bump on the head wouldn't slow Marcus Yolandi down for long, and once he raised the alarm - well, the clinic wasn't short on security.

She shook her head to clear the dizziness, and forced herself to run off down the corridor, her left arm hanging limp beside her. The other two followed. She struggled to work out the layout of the place. Somehow, they had to get to the back of the compound, but the whole place seemed to be built of just two templates; identical corridors and identical wards. Each time they turned a corner, they were presented with another long run of passageway. Each time they opened a door, a dark ward, filled with patients. Some lifted their heads to greet the newcomers with sunken eyes. Some shifted restlessly in their beds. Some groaned weakly in untreated pain. Laura, Dr. Dan, and Rochester ran on through and past then.

Suddenly, they skidded around a corner, and the corridor ended abruptly at a fire door. Laura pushed the bar down, and the door flew open. Instantly, an alarm sounded. They stumbled outside and looked around them in the blinding sunlight.

At the other side of the compound, Laura could see Marcus surrounded by a group of heavy looking men, still in their white coats. He was shouting orders at them, and they were sealing off the front gate. She flattened herself against the side of the building, and Dr. Dan and Rochester followed her lead.

Around the back of the building, the bins were just a few metres away. If they could just make it there without being seen, and if the bolt cutters were still there, and then if they could cut through the fence and get out before the guards caught up with them, then they stood a chance of getting out. Not a good chance, but a chance.

She gestured to the other two, and, keeping below the level of the windows, they crept along the wall. Laura's arm still throbbed with a dull ache, but at least the dizziness was gone for now. Laura looked back. Marcus was busy with his guards, pointing furiously, sending out groups of them to one area of the compound or another. Luckily nobody was looking towards the back of the clinic, yet.

She took her chance, and sprinted for the cover of the bins, diving behind them. The other two followed. Laura peered around. The bolt cutters were still there, leaning against the side of the dustbin.

"How fast can you cut through the fence?" she said to Dr. Dan. He looked at the fence. It was a good ten metres away, and once he got there, he would be in full view of anyone who cared to look. He shrugged.

"One way to find out, isn't there?" He grabbed the cutters and ran for the fence. Laura watched as he crouched down and started to cut through the wire. What had they done to her, she wondered. What was the poison spreading through her system? How long did she have?

She and Rochester positioned themselves behind the bins, and watched, poised like sprinters waiting for the gun. She saw him cut through one link, then another. He paused to pull the fence apart. A tiny hole had appeared. He cut again, and again, widening the gap.

Suddenly from the other side of the compound, a shout went up and all the guards turned to look. Yolandi had spotted the figure at the fence, and instantly everyone was running. Dr. Dan looked up, then frantically tore at the fence, trying to widen the hole enough to get through. Laura and Rochester launched themselves towards the gap.

There was the sound of a gun. Yolandi and his guards were running at full speed towards them. He held his pistol out in front of him, loosing off rounds as he ran. From the other side, another gang of guards were closing in.

Laura hit the fence hard, and was on her hands and knees in a second, scrambling through. Rochester followed as Dr. Dan held the fence open for him. Laura stood and turned in time to see Marcus raise his gun, only a few paces away from

Dr. Dan now. He was about to fire when Dr. Dan swung the bolt cutters, launching them directly at him. They hit him square in the face, and he dropped, the gun firing wildly at the same moment. Dr. Dan dived through the fence, and the three escapees pelted off across the road and between the rough tin shacks of the shanty town.

"Come on!" yelled Laura. "We can't stop here." Rochester had stopped. Hands on his knees.

"I'm too old for this," he said.

"They're not going to stop - we have to get to the car!" said Laura. Dr. Dan pulled Rochester up.

"Come on," he said. "Let's go." Reluctantly, he straightened.

"It's this way," said Rochester, and they started to pick their way through the maze of tightly packed buildings.

They dodged deeper into the mess of shacks, keeping away from the wider streets, and moving in the spaces between and behind. All around, they could hear shouting. The guards were combing through the streets, hunting them. At every corner, they paused, searched the streets and then scurried across into the cover of the far side, hearts pounding.

They clambered, wedged between two shacks lined with corrugated metal made burning hot by the sun. Right in front of them, in the street, a white coated guard passed by. Laura ducked instantly, the hot metal stinging her shoulder as she pressed against it. She almost cried out, but silenced herself. The guard ran on, and they crept out behind him, and across to the next piece of cover.

Slowly and silently, they made their way through the stinking city.

Eventually, Rochester hissed to her, and gestured to their left. Through a gap in the shacks, she could see the shape of the car.

"That's it?" whispered Dr. Dan, "we're supposed to get away in that heap of junk?"

Rochester frowned at him, "I'm sorry, "he said, "I left the private jet at the airport."

"Come on!" said Laura impatiently, and she stepped out into the road. About a hundred metres away, a guard spotted her immediately, shouted and started to run.

Rochester and Dr. Dan threw themselves out after Laura and the three pelted headlong towards the car. Laura looked back. Behind them, the guard was catching them. They would never make it.

Suddenly, a woman stepped from a shack in front of the guard, arms held out. Perhaps she thought he was looking for more test subjects and this was her chance. He brushed her aside, but as he turned, he slowed, and two men from another shack stepped out, grasping at him. He dodged into the path of an elderly woman and both went flying.

Laura ran on. When she looked back again, the guard was struggling to his feet, surrounded by grasping, pleading hands.

The three hit the car, and Rochester wrenched the door open. Dr. Dan climbed in next to him, and Laura struggled into the back. Rochester turned the key, spun the back wheels and the car bumped onto the dirt track.

"Don't let him drive!" Laura gasped, gulping for breath, but it was too late, the car skidded and jolted off down the road.

Laura looked out of the back window. The guard had finally got to his feet and was shouting into a radio. Behind him, other guards were emerging from the slums. Laura watched as they grabbed people from other vehicles still queuing to get to the clinic, and tossed them into the street. In a few seconds, two shabby cars, a motorbike and something that could once have been a school bus were in pursuit.

"It's not over," she shouted to Rochester in the front.

Rochester jammed his foot harder into the floor of the car and it jolted over a deep ridge of hardened mud. Up ahead, vehicles were still coming into town, spread out across both sides of the road, singing and waving. Laura gripped the seat in front of her as they accelerated straight into the path of the oncoming traffic. Rochester hit the horn, but it made little impact. Horns were going off in a wild celebration all around, and the vehicles heading towards them only swerved lazily to avoid collision when it became clear that Rochester was not changing his path.

They dodged left, and scraped the side of an already battered Citroen as it clattered past, forcing them onto the wrong side of the road. A solid looking pickup was rushing headlong towards them. Rochester yanked the steering wheel to avoid it, but it swerved the same way. He jerked it back even harder, and Laura was slammed across the seat into the right hand door. Already buckled, the door flew open and she grabbed onto the seat with one hand and the door with the other, toppling half in half out of the car.

She looked down. The road was rushing by below her.

She shifted her grip and hauled herself back in just as the pickup truck glanced the door, slamming it shut again with huge force.

Behind, their pursuers were closing. The school bus was in front, its radiator grill and lights filling the back window, grinning at Laura like a huge metal face. In front, the road was blocked. Two dusty, decorated trucks were traveling in parallel towards them, their drivers laughing with each other, apparently unaware of the rapidly shrinking road ahead.

Rochester drove straight at the few centimetres of gap between the two lorries. It was typical Rochester driving technique, thought Laura. He assumed they would get out of his way in preference to driving through him. On a London road, it would have worked, but he had not read the road correctly. On either side of the road, two other cars were overtaking the slow moving lorries. Even if the drivers saw them, they would have nowhere to go.

Laura closed her eyes and braced for the impact.

There was the sound of a skid and then a huge smash, but she felt nothing. She opened her eyes, and the two side windows were filled with walls of metal, millimeters away, but they were still moving. She looked back, disorientated. Behind, the gap between the lorries was plugged by the side of the school bus, sparking and sliding backwards.

The two drivers had spotted them, and parted just enough to let the car through. The bus chasing them hadn't been so lucky. It had swerved at the last moment and skidded, side-on into the front of the trucks, as they slowly ground to a halt.

Rochester, Dr. Dan and Laura shot out from between the lorries and into the mess of traffic trying to find a way to overtake them. They swerved left and then right and left again as Rochester tried to avoid them.

"Go off-road!" Laura shouted, and Rochester spun the car sideways and then hit the accelerator again, spraying up a plume of dirt before the wheels engaged, and they bumped off the road and onto flat, dusty scrubland.

Laura looked back. Behind them, the road was a mess of smoke and dust, and vehicles. It looked like there had never been a road, just a collection of toy cars randomly abandoned after a particularly destructive game. The two trucks and the bus were not going anywhere. Thick black smoke poured from the front of one, and the cars which had swerved to avoid their car were stalled at angles across the road. Meanwhile, other vehicles were slowly crawling off the road and making their way around the debris through clouds of thrown up dust and dirt.

As she watched, three vehicles emerged from the chaos, bumping across the dust towards them. The two cars were making heavy work of the ground, swerving and rocking from side to side as each wheel caught a different clod of earth or chunk of rock. The third vehicle was the motorbike. It tore around them, and dodged easily between rocks and bushes.

In just a few seconds, Laura could see it growing in the rear window. Its tyres were wide and spiked, and they dug into the ground as its rider weaved towards them. She could see him, helmetless on the back, still wearing his long, white coat which flapped behind him.

"Keep driving!" said Laura.

Rochester glared at her in the rear view mirror. "What did you think I was going to do?" he said.

By now, the motorcyclist was parallel with them, on the right hand side. She could see his face as he swung in towards them, and she could see the gun tucked into his belt. He couldn't take his hand off the handlebars to draw it, and on this rough terrain, he'd have no chance of hitting anything anyway.

He swooped past and in front of the car - hoping, Laura imagined, to slow them down, but Rochester's driving wasn't up to avoiding obstacles. He just carried straight on, barely missing the bike as it swerved in front of them. That wasn't going to work, Laura thought.

The rider, seemingly having the same thought, roared off ahead. About two hundred metres on, he skidded to a halt, turning the bike side on. He pulled the gun out and aimed at the oncoming car. Laura ducked as the side window beside her, and the back window simultaneously exploded. He was a good shot.

Rochester swerved, and the next bullet went wide. They were heading off at an angle now, making a wide circle around the bike. The rider waited until they were at their closest point, to him, and fired again.

The window next to Dr. Dan shattered, and he jerked suddenly in his seat. Rochester ploughed on away from the rider.

"Are you OK?" Laura said. Dr. Dan didn't answer. Laura leant over to where he was sitting, slumped in his chair. "Are you OK?" she said again, nudging him. He raised his hand. It was covered in blood. "Where?" she said. He gestured to his neck.

Laura peeled back the shirt from his shoulder. It was wet and red. The car was bumping and rocking as Rochester fought to keep it going. Eventually, she found the bullet hole. It was a deep gouge across the top of his shoulder.

"Just a scratch," she said. "You'll live." She pulled the shirt back over his wound to soak up the blood. Dr. Dan tried to grin. It didn't quite work. "What about me?" she said. Dr. Dan didn't answer, but the smile vanished.

"He's coming for another shot." said Rochester, watching through the rear view mirror. Laura looked around and out of the shattered back window. The rider was coming up fast and close behind them. He'd have to get ahead before he could fire. Laura looked back. Ahead was a clump of trees.

"Go through that!" she said. Rochester veered the car close to the trees just as the bike roared up to pass them. The rider was forced in close to the side of the car. At that second, Laura aimed both feet at the buckled back door. It flew open and the car juddered as the door caught the rider's front wheel and jammed it. The bike pitched, and the rider was thrown over the handlebars. Bike and door, wrenched sideways and disappeared in a cartwheel of twisted metal behind them.

Laura sat back. The door was gone, and she felt exposed as the scrubland blurred by outside.

The two pursuing cars were still following, and all the dodging and swerving meant that they were a lot closer now. They weren't giving up, but neither were built for this kind of landscape. As long as Rochester could keep up the pace, they wouldn't be able to get any closer.

Now it was just going to be about who made a mistake first. Laura thought that the odds were pretty good that it would be Rochester. She looked at him. He bumped the car through the landscape with his teeth gritted and his eyebrows permanently raised. There was no element of him that was settling to the task, and it was only a matter of time before he did something fatal.

Suddenly, the rocking slowed. The ground had evened out considerably. It was a road. Not smooth, not tarmacked, but very definitely a road. They swerved onto it, and picked up speed. Behind them, the other two cars did the same, but the road was narrow, and one had to drop back behind the other. Rochester, took the car up a gear, and steadied the steering. Dr. Dan's arm seemed to have stopped bleeding, and he was even able to get enough of a mobile signal to verify that they were heading in the general direction of the airfield.

Laura looked back. The flatter road was a relief, but it was not going to help them. On the flat, the other two cars were more powerful, and slowly, almost imperceptibly, they were gaining ground.

Rochester drove hard, but all the time, the other two cars were gaining. Within fifteen minutes, they were right behind them. Suddenly, Laura spotted a side-road. It was smaller than what served for the main path, and bore the tracks of heavy vehicles. It curved away, and out of sight down a hill. Laura signaled Rochester to take it, and they skidded off. Laura looked back. She had hoped the two cars would miss the turn and they would gain a little time, but both responded immediately, and were right on their tail.

They reached the brow of the hill, and Rochester instantly hit the brakes and spun the steering wheel. The car skidded round in a wide circle, sending stones flying into space. In front of them, the ground had simply vanished. The road turned sharply along a huge, manmade cliff face. A great scar had been carved out of the ground by open cast mining, and the road snaked down it, a circling, zig-zagging shelf of loose dirt and gravel, hugging an almost vertical drop hundreds of meters high.

At the bottom, huge tipper trucks were scattered like toys in a sand pit, and one mistake would send them crashing over the edge to join them. This was not a road for a driver like Melvin Rochester.

Behind them, the two cars were closing. Rochester hit the accelerator and they jerked forwards, skating more than driving down the loose gravel of the road. The first corner was a hairpin bend, and Rochester saw it late. He jammed on the brakes and spun the wheel, and the back end of the car lost all grip. It skidded in a huge arc around the corner. Laura saw the drop through the missing door and there seemed to be nothing between her and it. Rochester accelerated out of the corner, and the car straightened, wobbling on the gravel. Behind them, the two other cars followed.

The road tilted down, then snaked suddenly around an outcrop. Rochester barely corrected in time to avoid smashing straight into the vertical cliff. As it was, the headlamp was torn out by the rough rock and the whole car jumped sideways, the front bouncing out towards the drop on the other side. Rochester pulled the car in just in time, and then swerved around another tight bend. Behind them, the front car was so close, Laura could see the driver's face. He grinned at her, and hit the gas. The car surged forward, touching their back bumper, and shoving them faster down the track.

Rochester was breaking now. He could barely control the car, but the driver behind was accelerating, pushing them on, the wheels slipping. The path forked. One way went straight ahead, the other doubled back down the hill. Rochester swerved around, realised that they would never make the turn, and changed his mind, turning back onto the straight road.

For a long second, the two cars were next to each other, skidding sideways down a track barely wide enough to hold them. Then he steered hard, and the car straightened, sandwiching the pursuer against the rock face. He slowed enough for Rochester to pull away.

The road was even rougher now, less used, less repaired, but they ploughed on. There was one more hairpin bend before they reached the bottom of the pit and the ground levelled off, but suddenly, their pursuer hurled forwards, crashing straight into the back of them, and turning the car. They toppled straight over the edge of the road, and downwards. The mountain side sloped down at what felt like a vertical angle, but there was just enough gradient for Rochester to keep the wheels in touch with the rocky cliffside. They pitched downwards for probably twenty metres, and then the ground slowly levelled to form the bottom of the cliff. Behind them, the other two cars were making their way around the bend and down the road.

Rochester, shaking, caught his breath. They were ahead again.

He hit the accelerator - on solid, flat earth again, finally - and at that moment, the mountain exploded.

It started on the cliff, way behind and above them. Charges, wired to blow thousands of tonnes of rock for the miners to dig out. Laura saw the hillside shatter, and a cloud of dust billow outwards. The sound came a second later, low and rumbling. She watched as the explosions chased round the side of the mountain towards them. Detonations going off in sequence one after another.

"Drive!" she shouted. The car sped off, and Laura stared behind them as the explosion of raining rocks and smoke got closer and closer. The two vehicles struggling down the last stretch of cliffside road had no chance. They were engulfed and lost in a wave of smoke, and then from above, an entire mountainside of rock loosed itself from the cliff, and subsided into the cloud, rocks and boulders crashing and raining after it.

And still the explosions continued. The car picked up speed, but the chain of dynamite was faster. Explosions on the hillside got closer and closer until they were happening almost above the speeding car. Rochester kept driving. The cloud of smoke enveloped them, filling the car through the smashed windows, and he kept driving. Rocks and earth rained down on the roof, and he didn't stop. Suddenly, in front of them, a boulder the size of a house crashed down and crumbled instantly to fragments. Rochester skidded around it and kept going.

Suddenly, they were out of it. The dust cleared, the sound died away behind them, and the subsiding hillside calmed. The car bumped and hurtled past a small crowd of workers, staring in disbelief, and they took the only road out of the mine, alone.

It was not until they had almost reached the airfield that Marcus Yolandi finally caught up with them.

They had joined the track from the mine back to the main dirt road, and driven through a hundred miles of empty scrubland. Every few miles, they passed through a settlement, and Laura watched as crowds of children, playing in the street rushed out to wave to the passing car. She had turned, smiling to Rochester, and asked, "Why so many kids?"

"All the adults are dead," he had replied.

As they had driven on through the afternoon, Laura had felt the tiredness grow over her. Her arm felt like a soft, dead thing. Tender, and at the same time, without feeling. Something was making her feel nauseous, and she couldn't work out whether it was the heat, the poison, or the motion of the car. She drifted into a sleep, her head spinning.

"Call the pilot! Tell him to start the engine!" Rochester barked from the front seat. His phone landed in her lap, and jolted her fully awake. She looked around. It was beginning to get dark again, and the car was speeding through the town just outside the airfield. Behind them, a jeep was tearing along the road. Inside, she could see Marcus Yolandi and Sylvia Gryene.

"He must have guessed this was where we were heading," said Dr. Dan.

Laura phoned through, and gave the pilot his instructions. He would be on the runway when they got there. Marcus was closing on them, but there was nothing to be done. It was one straight road to the airfield. No shortcuts. If they took a detour, he would just be there waiting for them when they arrived. Laura looked around. Maybe there was something to throw at them.

The car was empty. She pulled at the seat beside her. Nothing was loose except for the headrest. She yanked it hard, it came off in her hand. A faux leather cushion supported on two solid metal spikes. She waited until the jeep had caught up, then hurled it out of the hole where the back window had been. The spikes struck the window of the jeep, and it instantly crazed with a pattern of tiny, opaque fractures. The car skidded, swerved and fell back. Marcus smashed his fist through the broken glass, and swept the smashed fragments out of the way before accelerating after them.

It had brought them a little time. Up ahead, the gates of the airfield were firmly shut. The smiling man whose car they had hired and virtually destroyed was sitting reading a paper in the window of his office. He looked up just in time to see his ruined vehicle smash through the gate, sending it flying off its hinges, and screech to a halt on the runway next to the throbbing engines of the plane.

Rochester leapt out, and pulled Laura from the back seat. Dr. Dan struggled out, still holding his wounded arm, and they all ran for the aircraft. The two men half carried, half dragged Laura up the steps towards the doorway just as Marcus's jeep skidded through the gates. He launched himself out of the vehicle, drawing his gun and letting off three wild shots which pinged off the aircraft steps.

Rochester dived through the door, dragged Laura after him, and Dr. Dan climbed over both, pushing the steps up to seal the door behind him. Outside, they heard one more shot before the engine noise grew suddenly to a roar, flooding out all other sound, and the aircraft picked up speed, powering down the runway, and lifting gently into the sky.

The three clambered to the window and looked down as the plane banked around the airport to set its course for home.

Down below, Laura could see the furious Marcus, staring up. But just before the plane roared off towards the north, she saw something else - another plane. Another private jet, taxiing onto the runway behind them ready to take off, and their two pursuers running towards it.

Chapter 22: Flying Doctors

"Are you going to tell me what they injected me with?" Laura asked. Dr. Dan moved away from the plane window, but didn't say anything.

"Come on, man," said Rochester, sinking into a white leather seat. "Let's hear what we're dealing with!"

Dan Pan took a deep breath. "Well, I don't know the concentration -"

"But?" said Laura.

"And I can't be sure what else is in it -"

"Out with it!" said Rochester.

"Deadly Nightshade," said Dr. Dan.

Laura slumped into her seat. Her arm was throbbing. Her mind raced back to Dr. Dan's grinning description of the symptoms at the factory; headaches, delirium, hallucinations, rashes, dizziness, convulsions, he had happily told her. And then death. She remembered his smile. "And then death," he had said in the tone of voice he might have used for "and then ice cream."

He was not smiling now.

"You need to rest," said Dr. Dan. He adjusted her seat so she was lying flat.

"Rest?" she said, her head beginning to spin. Her mouth felt suddenly dry. "Is that all you've got? You're supposed to be the best doctor on television, and you're telling me to have a lie down?" Dr. Dan looked at the floor. "Is there a cure?" said Laura.

Dr. Dan and Rochester looked at each other. "An antidote," Dr. Dan corrected. "There is an antidote. Physostigmine. It's another poison," he added, helpfully.

"Great," said Laura. "Where do we get it?"

"Not on this plane" said Dr. Dan, abruptly. "She needs a hospital. Come to think of it, I wouldn't mind one myself." He touched his shoulder and winced slightly.

"Well we don't have one!" snapped Rochester. Laura thought of the thick drops of liquid dripping from the vat of nightshade in the factory. The technician, masked and gloved lest a drop touch his skin. And now that stuff was in her blood, flowing around her body. Her heart. Her brain. And it wasn't some homeopathic preparation - a drop loosed into a vat of water, and then a drop from that diluted again and again. The liquid in the syringe had been thick and dark.

She pictured it flowing through her veins. It must have invaded her whole body by now, and now that the danger of being shot was over, for now, and all she could do was lie back and wait, she started to feel the poison doing its work. What had Dr. Dan said? Headaches? Now that she thought of it, her head did hurt. It hurt a lot. She had put it down to tiredness, but, no. The sickness she felt in the car was back, and it was worse, turning her stomach over and over. She closed her eyes, and her brain was on a rollercoaster. Above her, the two men were arguing. She tried to focus on their voices.

"We need to land!" Rochester was saying.

"We can't! We have to get her home!" said Dr. Dan.

"You're still trying to get her to the rally?" Rochester was appalled, "You're reckless!"

"No!" shouted Dr. Dan.

"Look at her. She'll never make it!" Shouted Rochester.

"I can do this!" Laura mumbled, struggling to sit up. Rochester pushed her down again.

"You're just using her" said Rochester. "You have been from the start. Face it, it's over!"

"It's not that!" said Dr. Dan.

"What then?" said Rochester.

"If we land now, we'd have to declare it was an emergency landing."

"So?" Rochester said.

"Medics would meet us at the plane," said Dr. Dan

"Good!"

"But Marcus would land right beside us. What chance do you think we'd have?" asked Dr. Dan. "If we carry on to London, it's just a standard landing at a busy airport - we might just get out and to a hospital before he finds us."

Laura looked up at them. Rochester was thinking hard. He turned and strode off towards the cabin "How fast can this plane go?" he boomed. Laura looked back at Dr. Dan.

"How long have I got?" she said. He shook his head.

"We don't know the dose," he paused. "Just hold on," he said grimly.

The hours passed. Laura drifted. Sometimes asleep, sometimes awake. Mostly, in the half aware no man's land between the two. Often she stared out of the window, and saw, or imagined she saw, another white shape shadowing their journey. Marcus and Granny Gryene were following. She knew that, but did she see them or just think she did? There was no way to be sure.

She was aware of the two doctors, sometimes lifting her hand to feel her pulse, sometimes holding a hand to her forehead to test her temperature, sometimes on the other side of the plane, talking in low voices. They argued in a tone that implied the conversation was about her, but in words too low to catch.

"Maybe..." one said, "we could try...." But she couldn't hear who said it, or what came next. The other seemed dismissive - "It would never work!" She drifted away from them again.

When she woke, they were both standing over her. She could feel a great pressure on her chest as though hands were pressing down on her, squeezing the life out of her. She tried to move, but all she could do was open and close her mouth. Dr. Dan was holding her wrist, feeling for a pulse. His face creased with concern.

"It's all over the place." he said, and he handed her wrist to Rochester, who felt it himself. He too looked grave. "We have to try it," said Dr. Dan. Rochester sighed and then nodded.

Dr. Dan ran towards the cockpit and returned with a tiny glass, filled with cloudy orange liquid. He held it to her lips. It tasted thick, and strangely sweet. A soon as she swallowed, it burned in her throat. She coughed.

"What is it?" she managed.

Dr. Dan and Rochester exchanged glances.

"You have to drink it all," said Dr. Dan. Then he added, "It'll steady your heart." The two men looked at each other again. Rochester held her wrist.

"It's working." he said. He did not sound sure. Then, again, more definitely. "Yes, it's working."

Laura started to breathe more regularly, and now that Rochester had said it, she did feel calmer. The pressure on her chest was reducing. She was about to ask again what the mixture was, when she felt the drowsiness flow over her again, and she closed her eyes.

It felt like a second later, when her eyes flicked open to the sensation of a sudden jolt.

"It's OK," said Dr. Dan beside her. "We've landed." The plane taxied to a halt, and Rochester flung the doors open.

"We have to get to the car," he said. "Can you make it?" Laura nodded. Her legs felt like they could snap, but there was no option. Dr. Dan helped her to her feet, and they struggled down the stairs onto the runway. Rochester's car had been driven out to meet them, and she was maneuvered into the back.

As Rochester jammed his foot on the gas pedal, and they pulled evenly away, Laura watched another small jet skidding in to land a short way off. Marcus Yolandi was back in England just minutes behind them.

Chapter 23: A Very Homeopathic Poison

The emergency nurse looked back and forth between Dr. Dan Pan and Dr. Melvin Rochester.

"Atropine poisoning?" she said.

"From deadly nightshade," said Rochester.

"How many berries did she eat?" said the nurse.

"It was" - Dr. Dan hesitated. "It was injected," he said. "So we don't know." The nurse looked incredulously at them.

"- And you say you've been shot?"

"Don't worry about me." said Dr. Dan.

"I think we'll decide for ourselves who to worry about," said the nurse, sternly. "When did this happen?"

"About sixteen hours ago." said Rochester.

"And what treatment has been given so far?"

"Nothing," said Rochester. The nurse stared from one famous doctor to the other and back.

"Nothing?" she said. Dr. Dan and Rochester shook their heads.

"She needs physostigmine urgently!" said Rochester.

The nurse stared at him. "Quite possibly!" she said coldly. "Wait here!" she rushed out.

Laura struggled to sit up. "Why didn't you tell them?" she said. The walk from the car had made her very weak. She could feel her heart pounding in her chest. It felt wrong. Out of time.

"Tell them what?" said Rochester.

"What you gave me in the plane," she said, "You told her there had been no treatment." Rochester shifted uncomfortably and stared at Dr. Dan.

"There wasn't," said Dr. Dan eventually. He sighed, "I just mixed up some orange juice and sweeteners with some vodka from the bar."

"What?" said Laura, "Why?"

He shrugged, "A placebo. If you think you're being treated, it can improve your symptoms," he said. "It couldn't cure you, but you relaxed and that brought us some time."

"You tricked me," she said, "but I really did feel better!" Dr. Dan shrugged.

"It wasn't my idea," said Rochester.

Laura's chest thumped. It suddenly felt tight again. All the time she had thought Dr. Dan's medicine was helping, she had been able to move. Now, she realised she hadn't been treated at all. There was nothing working against the poison flooding her system. Her breathing started coming in short bursts. The room tipped and pitched around her. Her legs gave way without warning.

Through the dizzying chaos, she saw Rochester and Dr. Dan run from the room shouting. A few seconds later, they returned, another doctor appeared behind them. He held up a bottle and a syringe. Dr. Dan and Rochester held her arm, while the new doctor lifted the bottle, pierced it and drew a quantity of pure liquid.

Dr. Dan dabbed her arm with a cotton wool swab. The room was spinning around her. The doctor leaned in with the hypodermic poised.

Instantly the door burst open, and a hand reached over the doctor's shoulder, pulling him backwards. It was an old hand. Wrinkled skin and manicured nails.

The doctor spun backwards, and behind him, Laura saw Granny Gryene.

"Leave her!" she shouted. Dr. Dan and Rochester twisted around, and grabbed her by the arms, hauling her out of the way, and the bemused doctor turned back towards Laura, bringing the needle down towards her arm. "Stop! You don't understand!" Granny Gryene shouted. The doctor paused.

Now Granny Gryene spoke directly to her granddaughter, "Get up, dear," she said, "I switched the syringe. There's nothing wrong with you!"

Laura stared in disbelief. If there was no poison, why was her head spinning? Why was her heart thumping? Why were the doctors convinced that she was at the point of death?

The hospital doctor drew back. "I don't know what kind of game you're playing here!" he said, "but this injection could have killed you." He stormed out of the room.

Laura clambered, gasping to her feet. Dr. Dan and Rochester released Granny Gryene and were staring at her.

"But her symptoms -" said Dr. Dan eventually.

"Were entirely based on your description of them!" said Rochester. "You told her how a victim of belladonna poisoning should respond. She believed she had been poisoned, and her body reacted accordingly!"

Laura gaped. "That's impossible!" she said.

"Really?" said Rochester. "A moment ago, you couldn't stand. Now suddenly, you can." she looked down at her legs. He was right, and she could feel her heartbeat slowly returning to normal.

After a moment, she said, "Tell me one thing: if I hadn't found out, would I have died?"

Rochester and Dr. Dan looked at each other. Sylvia Gryene brushed herself down, and straightened her suit.

"Am I to understand that you were about to give my granddaughter poison?" she demanded.

"We were about to give her the proper treatment for her symptoms!" retorted Rochester.

"Which would have killed her!" snorted Laura's grandmother. "Typical conventional medicine." She turned to Laura, "Shall we go, dear?" she said.

"Where is your friend?" said Rochester.

"He is not my friend, you odious man!" said Granny Gryene, sharply. "He's quite mad. I have seen his operation and I want no part of it. I have severed my links with him."

"You're as guilty as he is!" shouted Rochester. "Your industrial quackery created him!" The two glared at each other across the room.

"He's a madman - nothing else," she said. "I've managed to send him to the wrong hospital looking for you, but he will come after us. We need to get away from here, and let the police pick him up at the rally. That's where he thinks you're going."

"Shut up, both of you," snapped Laura.

Dr. Dan stepped between them. He looked at the clock on the wall, and spoke directly to Laura, "The rally is in an hour," he said. "Your grandfather set this up. You are the only person who can follow it through." Sylvia Gryene rolled her eyes.

"You can't still be pursuing this silliness!" she said, "I had great respect for your grandfather, and it broke my heart that he wanted to do this to me. But you have to understand, by the end, he had changed. He had lost himself," she paused, her eyes wet. "The drugs..."

Laura swung around and glared at her. "He wasn't taking any drugs!" she said.

"He would never have intended all this," she said. "You must know that."

"You can't listen to her!" shouted Rochester.

"Come on!" said Laura, looking from Granny Gryene to Dr. Dan and then to Rochester. "Let's go!" She stepped towards the door.

"Laura," said Granny Gryene, "your parents are with the vet right now. They're preparing to go to the sanctuary and destroy the animals." Laura stopped in her tracks. She felt her heart drop into her stomach. Dead Cat Day. Now. She was not ready. Granny Gryene put her hand on Laura's shoulder. "You have to be with your family now."

Laura pushed her hand away, but did not move.

"What are you going to do?" said Rochester. "This has to be your decision."

Laura stood in the doorway. There was silence.

"We have to get Christof," she said. She looked at Granny Gryene. "All of us," she said.

"And then what?" said Rochester.

"I don't know." Laura walked out, the other three others following.

Chapter 24: Dead Cat Day

"Shut up!" Laura sat in the back of the car with Christof on her lap. They were parked up and looking across the road at her home. "Shut up!" she said again. Rochester and Sylvia Gryene had been bickering in the front all the way. It was frighteningly familiar. She and Grandad had argued in exactly the same way, only now, Laura could not stand to hear it.

They had picked up Christof on the way. Samuel had handed him over, with, what Laura thought was a surprising degree of reluctance. He had stroked the cat's head, and waved an effete little goodbye with his fingers before straightening up, and appearing to notice the strange collection of celebrities and gunshot victims who had filed into the shop.

"You've become very famous, you and your cat," he had said. "Is it true you know Christof Tourenski?" Laura had gritted her teeth, and shrugged. If she didn't show up at the rally, and left Grandad's plan unfinished, then this would be her life from now on. A joke without a punchline.

"It's complicated," she had said.

He had looked suddenly serious, "What have you got yourself into?" she had not answered. "Is it something I can help with?" he had said.

He was only trying to help, she thought, and there was something comforting about that. People who were just simply on her side without their own sinister plans for her were pretty thin on the ground these days. She decided

Samuel had earned a place on her "people to trust" list after all once Dead Cat Day and the Rally were both safely in the past. Assuming she survived that long.

Then she caught herself mid thought - there was a difference between being trustworthy and being reliable, or stable. She had no idea what she was going to do next, but whatever it was, it wasn't going to involve a semi-psychotic gun obsessed freak. One of those was quite enough to deal with.

Across the road, the front door opened. The vet was dressed in his turquoise overalls. Clean and freshly ironed. It was a special occasion, and he had clearly made an effort. In his hand, a small, grey case. On his face, the tight grim smile of the executioner. He walked briskly to the car. No reason to waste time.

A second after him, Judy, and Peter. They followed slowly, Peter stooping. Judy holding his arm. Like pensioners at a funeral, defeated and broken. They followed the vet to the car. Judy climbed inside. Peter paused, and took one last long look up and down the street. Laura knew what he was looking for. He was looking for her. Waiting for her to come and fulfil her promise. For a moment, he seemed to be staring straight into the car window, straight into her eyes, but he was not. He saw the reflection on the car window. Nothing more. After a long moment, he gave up and started to clamber laboriously into the car. "I've got an idea," she had told him in their last conversation. A lie she had hoped to make true.

But that was before. Before the chase through the dusty land with its villages of motherless children. Before the clamouring at the gates of the clinic. Before the endless hopeless beds.

"Go to them," said Granny Gryene.

"You don't care about this," said Laura. "You never did."

"I care about my son," she said, her voice softening, "and he needs you."

"You could have stopped this! They just needed money."

"I could have delayed it, maybe," she said.

Dr. Dan looked at his watch, "You can't do anything now," he said.

"I can be there," said Laura, "I promised them."

"You parents will understand," said Dr. Dan, but it wasn't her parents she had promised. It was another promise. Made silently by tearing up a sticker. Did that matter? A promise made to a kitten? After everything she had seen, did that still matter?

And there was the question. What matters more? The big thing that you cannot do, or the small thing you can? Holding down eighty cats while they were put to death so her parents did not have to watch, or being Grandad's punchline in front of a madman with a gun and a thousand people who did not want to hear the joke.

Either way, today was not going to end well.

Across the road, the car started up, and trundled reluctantly out of the drive. Suddenly, at the other end of the street, another car screeched around the corner. Dark, and square-fronted. Marcus Yolandi was on to them.

Laura's parents' car was pulling away, but the other car had spotted them, and was accelerating.

"He must think that's us!" said Laura, "Go now!"

Rochester spun the wheel and the car moved off in a wide arc, just scraping the rear of Marcus' car as it sped past. Laura just caught sight of him turning and recognising her. As the dark car twisted, its driver distracted, the front hit a parked car on the other side of the road. Rochester continued his smooth one hundred and eighty degree turn while Marcus, accelerated backwards down the road after them.

Looking back, Laura just glimpsed her parents' and the vet turning slowly out of sight at the other end of the road. Peter, no connoisseur of the rear view mirror, had not noticed a thing.

"Where are we going?" Rochester yelled.

"Parliament Square," said Laura without thinking, and they turned onto the main road towards the bridge. Behind them, Marcus shot backwards out of the turning, into traffic, spun the car to face them and jolted forwards.

Rochester jammed his foot on the accelerator. Up ahead, the road to the bridge was choked with ponderous London buses. If anything, the car slowed. Its detectors had spotted the mess of traffic in front of them and saw no reason for speed. In Laura's lap, Christof, popped his head up, and peered out of the back window. His assassin was gaining.

Ahead, a bus swung in towards the kerb to pick up passengers, and a gap, only slightly narrower than the car, opened up. Rochester pointed the car at it. Proximity alarms sounded from the dashboard, and the car hesitated, but he forced it forward and eventually the vehicle accepted its fate. Oncoming traffic crowded in. The bus to the side started to pull out. The one directly in front trundled on and Rochester steered to undertake it. Presented with imminent collision from every angle, the car's safety features went to war with each other. The car jerked, bumped and wove as Rochester piloted it between busses and cyclists. Behind them, Marcus' much wider car was trapped, unable to follow. Laura glimpsed it screeching to a halt and veering off down a side street looking, no doubt for some other way to intercept them.

Rochester's car burst suddenly out of the traffic, onto a roundabout which Rochester utterly ignored. Car horns exploded from every incoming road as they glided across and onto Lambeth Bridge. They zig-zagged across, between busses and cyclists, and turned onto the final stretch down towards parliament.

It was instantly clear they would have to continue on foot. Ahead, the road was blocked by a police cordon, about a thousand people, and a travelling falafel salesman. The rally had started.

Rochester jammed on the brakes, sending Christof toppling into the footwell. He veered into a side street and cut the engine. Granny Gryene leapt out of the car, and Dr. Dan struggled out after her. Rochester followed.

By the time Laura got hold of Christof and clambered out of the car, Granny Gryene had rushed off around the corner. They found her addressing a policeman.

"He's trying to kill my granddaughter... "she was saying. Laura pulled her away.

"What are you doing?" Laura demanded.

"I'm trying to save your life!" she said. By now, the other two had caught up with them. The policeman manning the cordon looked at Rochester, Dr. Dan, and Laura. This was clearly beyond his pay-grade. Another two policemen on the other side of the road were beginning to show interest.

Laura thought quickly. Once they spotted Dr. Dan's bloodstained shirt, this would become a manhunt and they would be tied up asking questions for hours. Granny Gryene may have been trying to protect her, but she was clever enough to know she would also be making certain Laura would never get to the rally.

"This is my grandmother," said Laura to the policemen. "She's a bit confused. She watches a lot of television...." The policeman smiled with relief, and nodded, waving them on. She could feel Granny Gryene glaring at her as she ran on towards Big Ben, but when she checked behind, all three were still following her.

Parliament Square had been sectioned off from the road by tall, wooden barricades for the rally. Laura could not see over them, but she could hear the sounds of a crowd from the other side. The only break in the barricade was a curtained entrance. Looking through, she could see steps leading up to the speaker's stage. This was where she needed to be.

"We can't go with you," said Dr. Dan behind her. "Everyone in there knows our faces. We would blow the whole thing."

"I'll make sure Marcus doesn't get in," said Rochester.

"I'll see if I can see him in the crowd," said Dr. Dan.

Laura watched the elderly Rochester park himself as discreetly as he could near the flimsy canvas door, and the injured Dr. Dan trying to painfully squeeze himself through the barrier. If she had been choosing bodyguards, they wouldn't have been top of her list. She stepped towards the curtain.

"I'm coming with you," said Granny Gryene. "They'll know me," Laura looked at her. This old lady wouldn't be much help in a fight even if Laura could work out which side she was on.

"You can't let her in there with you!" said Rochester, putting an arm on her shoulder.

"Get your hand off me," said Granny Gryene, glaring at him. He removed the hand reluctantly.

"She still wants to stop you," said Rochester.

"Yes, I do," she said. "You're making a fool of yourself, and I want to protect you,"

"For all we know she's still working with Yolandi," he said.

"Don't be absurd, you stupid man!" snapped Granny Gryene. Laura watched the two, bickering. It was like a flashback to every family gathering she could remember. Grandad and Granny Gryene fighting. She left them to it and slipped in behind the curtain.

"So pleased you could make it. We were beginning to worry," It was Geraldine Hartley, the Minister for Health. She grabbed Laura's free hand and shook it hard. "Still have the famous cat I see! Wonderful!" She grinned. "They're almost ready for you up top," she gestured up a set of metal stairs. Christof sniffed at her hand, and didn't appear to like it much.

"Right," Laura said, as confidently as she could manage.

From the inside, Laura could see that the stage was created from the side of a lorry, with scaffolding and canvas erected around it to protect the speakers (although, not, she quickly noted, from a bullet). On the ground level, a couple of weedy looking interns with t-shirts and clipboards wandered about checking things. If they all got together, they could probably hold back an angry aromatherapist. At the top of the stairs, Laura could see sky. The stairs lead to the right, through a wooden door into a small waiting area, and to the left directly out onto the stage.

"There's a good crowd," said the Minister. "I've already done my little bit, but it's you they really want to see - you and Christof." Laura looked up towards the stage. The crowd might be waiting for her now, but by the time she had finished speaking, she thought, she would probably be a lot less popular. She had not given a lot of thought to what her life would be like if she survived this. She wondered if Grandad had. The whole plan suddenly seemed foolish. Could she really go through with this?

"What do you mean, your little bit?" she said.

"I've told them we're with them at the Ministry," said the Minister. "I think it's finally time - with public opinion behind us, we can really start rolling alternative therapy out across the whole health system. The public don't just want to be given what scientists say is right - they want a choice of treatments. With advocates like Christof behind us, I really think today could be a turning point."

Laura shuddered, and then turned to the stairs. It was time to face the music.

She had got to the fourth step before Hartley called out after her. "He's already up there waiting for you."

Laura froze. "Who?" She said.

"Why, Christof, of course!" said the Minister. "Up you go." Laura pushed open the door, slowly, but she knew who she would find in the small, dark waiting room. Marcus turned and smiled.

"I think this has all gone far enough, don't you?" he said. His hand was in his jacket pocket, covering the gun he undoubtedly held there. "Close the door." Laura obeyed as slowly as she could.

Behind her, she could hear a commotion downstairs. The minister's voice was raised, but Laura couldn't hear what she was saying.

"You're not going to get away, you know," said Laura.

"Do you know how many people there are out there?" he laughed. "I could sit down with a picnic in front of Big Ben and the police wouldn't find me."

"Why are you doing this? You know the pills don't work," she said.

Marcus shrugged, "It's just business," he said, simply. "It's not about what you know, is it? It's about what you believe. All I'm doing is helping people who want to believe."

"But I'm not the only one who knows about you." she said.

"Yes, your Grandfather has made quite a mess, hasn't he?" he said. "I will have to start my trials again somewhere else with more volunteers. Luckily, there is no shortage of those," he laughed. "By the time your friends return, the clinic will have moved, and I will have a new name. They will just sound like what they are - celebrities with an axe to grind."

Laura could hear feet on the stairs behind her now. If she could just delay him for a few seconds. She stepped away from the door. "How do you know we haven't got evidence?"

Marcus laughed dismissively, "Evidence?" He said. "Do you think anyone cares about evidence?" he paused. "The only person who could cause me any trouble is your grandmother, but I'm sure I can find one old woman." Marcus pulled the gun out of his pocket, and levelled it at her. His finger tightened.

Suddenly, everything seemed to happen at once. Laura heard the door burst open and turned to see Granny Gryene burst into the room, with Rochester in pursuit. A smile spread across Marcus' face. The gun jolted in his hand as he pulled the trigger. Laura felt an instant impact from the side, as Granny Gryene barged her out of the path of the bullet.

Rochester flew across the room and delivered a single, solid punch to the side of Marcus's head. The man spun with the impact, and his head collided with the jutting end of a scaffolding pipe. He collapsed instantly to the ground, out cold.

Laura looked back towards Granny Gryene. She was staggering, looking down at her stomach. Red blood was running through her fingers. Rochester was at her side, catching her as she fell to the floor.

"Is it bad?" she said, the colour draining with every second from her face.

Rochester looked down at the wound. He put his hand over it, slowly, and looked up. "It's fine," he said, finally. "Nothing to worry about." He looked at Laura. It was not fine. Not in any way. Rochester coughed, "A couple of glasses of pomegranate juice and you'll be right as rain."

"Don't patronise me!" said Granny Gryene, managing a weak laugh. She looked at Laura, "Well, go on then!" She said. "Do what you have to do."

"But the factory is your life's work," said Laura.

She shook her head, "No," she said, "you were." She struggled to sit up, "your Grandad and I argued about almost everything," she said. "Why would we expect you to agree with either of us?"

An arm suddenly reached through the door, and grabbed Laura's elbow. She turned to see one of the clipboard-wielding interns.

"Ready?" said the girl, perhaps a couple of years older than herself. From where she was standing, she could not see the three people lying on the floor of the room. Laura glanced back. Granny Gryene had her eyes closed, and had slumped back. Rochester looked up, shaking his head.

"Ready." She stepped out onto the stage, and the girl gestured towards a microphone in the centre. Laura stumbled towards it, still looking back at the door behind which her grandmother lay dead. It was not until she reached the centre that she became aware of the deafening roar of the crowd. She stopped to stare out at them.

When Geraldine Hartley had said there was a good crowd, Laura had assumed she meant a couple of thousand people.

She had not. A couple of thousand people more or less would have made no difference at all to the throng crowded into Parliament Square. The attendees of the garden party had mobilised their forces and gathered their army, and the results were extraordinary. All the disparate factions of the alternative medicine industry had temporarily forgotten their substantial differences and called their supporters to lobby with one simple demand - to be taken seriously.

A multicoloured sea of people were crowded in front of the stage. But these were just the eager ones who had arrived early and fought their way to the front. They had painted their faces, and prepared banners: "Stop poisoning our children!" read one alongside a photo of a baby's bottle filled with pills. "Vaccines cause autism!" bellowed another. "Fight the pharmaceutical conspiracy" a third proclaimed.

Behind this vanguard, the grass of Parliament square was filled. Families with young children, students sitting in circles, seasoned campaigners whose wrinkled faces had clearly been to every protest march since the sixties. They crowded into groups, chatting, chanting, eating street food, and enjoying the atmosphere of good-natured, harmless protest.

Further back, latecomers were still filing along past the wide, impressively architectured government buildings of Whitehall into the square, in a flow of people to which Laura could not see an end. Some had clambered up onto the statues that surrounded the square. Winston Churchill, Gandhi, and Lincoln all had spectators perched on them craning for a better view.

The microphone whined in echoing feedback, and Christof squirmed in her arms. The crowd calmed. Waiting.

It was at this point that Laura realised that she had no idea whatsoever what she was going to say. The time Grandad had probably intended her to spend preparing her speech had been mainly taken up with trying not to die, and now, in front of this massive and eager audience, she had nothing. She stared, wide eyed out into the crowd, and felt terror, and Christof, clawing their way up from her belly to her throat.

At the side of the stage, she could see Rochester standing in the doorway. Dr. Dan had appeared beside him. He nodded at her. Her throat was dry. Her heart pumping.

Finally she held up her cat in both hands above her head. He hung there, front paws stuck straight out, back legs dangling.

"This is Christof Tourenski!" she said. The crowd let out a slightly confused "Ahhh..." Laura could see, in amongst them, a few faces react instantly to Christof. Heads turning. Eyes focused. Each one, strangely obvious to Laura even as faces in a crowd. She recognised them instantly. The Cat People were out in force.

Laura started again. "Christof Tourenski is a cat!" Another, quieter cheer. The Cat People were enraptured now. Their eyes sparkling, following Christof. They understood instantly - or thought they did. Christof

Tourenski - the famous cat-guru! Everyone else was looking increasingly confused. This approach was going nowhere.

She put Christof down, holding his leash, and grabbed the microphone from its stand. Enough with the grand gestures, she thought. She started to tell her story.

She talked about her grandfather and how she had seen him die. She talked about Christof, and how she had been so taken in by his experiences and his qualifications, only to discover that they were all worthless.

She talked about the factory, and the strange rituals of making pills out of infinitely diluted poisons. She told them about the horrors of the clinic, and the desperate, dying people, and how she, herself had been so convinced that she was poisoned that it had almost killed her.

By the time she had finished, her fear was gone. She was alone on the stage, just telling her story, and a part of her had forgotten that her audience were even there. When she finally stopped, and looked out over them, she realised that she had lost them.

Perhaps Grandad had hoped that the impact of the punchline would be enough to puncture the euphoria. Christof Tourenski was a cat, and everything that followed from that would be obvious to all. The pure ridiculousness of it would be enough to carry the message echoing across the world.

It was not.

The crowd were not there to hear that story. They were there to hear another, simpler one. "Know your audience," That was what Grandad had always told her. "Know what they want to hear, and give them that." But he had failed to hear his own advice. Being dead will do that for you.

In the end, Grandad's message was too complicated to be delivered from a podium. In the end, a distorted PA was an insufficient delivery mechanism to put across what she had to say to a crowd of half listening, half partying people who just did not want to hear it.

Probably most of them knew in their hearts already that the whole thing was shot through with fraud and self-deception. Just less so, they imagined, than what it was pitted against. Probably they knew that there was no magic that could cure the ills of their mad lifestyles. Probably most of them weren't even looking for a cure. They were looking for a conspiracy to blame, and a day out in the sun, and a placebo they could believe in. And who could blame them for that?

In the end, she was just a mad girl standing on a stage waving a cat with a funny name. And in the end, Grandad was not a master puppeteer playing one last impossible joke from beyond the grave. He was just a dying man taking a desperate shot at getting even, and not quite pulling it off.

Only the Cat People were still staring, but even they were only listening to the words they wanted to hear. They were staring at Christof, and building their own stories around him. Even at a distance, she could see it in their eyes. Laura stopped. A few of the crowd jeered. A few of them weakly applauded. Most just carried on chatting, or chanting, or dancing, or staring at Christof the guru-cat.

It was over. She looked to Dr. Dan and Rochester, and shrugged helplessly. The moment was gone. The press would lead with the photo of her holding her cat in the air "Christof Tourenski is a cat" would be the headline, but what that really meant would be lost. There was nothing more to be done.

Or was there? Perhaps there was something. Perhaps, some little thing - perhaps out of all this, there was just one promise she could keep after all.

She looked back to the audience. The disinterest was palpable. Everyone but the Cat People had abandoned her.

She pulled her mobile from her pocket, flicked up Samuel's number, and hit dial. She threw the phone to Dr. Dan.

"Tell him to get to the sanctuary," she said, covering the microphone, "tell him to barricade the doors until we get there. Tell him to do whatever it takes to defend the place!" Dr. Dan looked puzzled, but put the phone to his ear.

Laura turned back to the crowd, and picked up Christof, and held him up to her face. In the crowd, the Cat People's eyes followed their idol, until they were looking at her face again. She ignored the rest of the confused crowd, and spoke directly to the Cat People. "Know your audience," Grandad had told her. And this was an audience Laura knew.

Chapter 25: Weapon of Choice

Laura looked back. Nearly there. Behind her there was quite a procession. About five hundred, or so Cat People had responded to her plea, and were following her to the cat's home on foot. Around her, the press buzzed like flies.

They had crossed the bridge already and were heading down into the back streets of Lambeth. Somewhere behind, the rally was breaking up. Rochester was trying to calm the Minister for Health, whose reaction to finding, two bodies, one dead, and one, live but unconscious with a head wound and a gun, backstage was not a pleasant one. Dr. Dan was dealing with the police. His trademark smile being stretched to its limit, both diplomatically and physically.

But for Laura, there was a strange feeling of elation. Finally, she was in control. She had a plan. For the first time since the funeral, she knew what was going on even if nobody else had a clue, and she had an army behind her. Even if it was a tatty, misguided and slightly mad one. There were easily enough cat people to empty the home of its residents, and she knew she could rely on Samuel to keep the vet and her parents out until they arrived. This might even work.

There would be a mess to clean up afterwards. A pretty big mess, involving court cases, funerals, the world's press, and quite possibly the Ugandan police. Not to mention the fact that she would come out owning a defunct cat's home and a homeopathic medicine factory. She would probably need to run away and change her name. And then there was the clinic. Without Marcus Yolandi, what would happen to that? But that mess was for tomorrow. Right now, it felt fantastic to know where she was going and why.

The feeling lasted for about fifteen seconds. Then her phone rang. It was Samuel.

"I'm in," he said grimly, "the place is in lock-down. Nobody's getting in." Laura felt he sounded a little too combative. A little too cocky. Then he added, "I found something in one of the cages. I've taken it. I hope you don't mind." he rang off.

The gun.

In all the chaos, she had forgotten about the gun hidden under the Boston Strangler's bedding. Laura crumpled inside. She had told the guy most likely to be involved in a shoot-out to instigate a siege, and she had given him a loaded gun.

She started to run.

She took the crowd of journalists and cameramen following her by surprise, but they soon picked up speed. She lengthened her stride. Whatever happened next, it would be better for it not to be recorded, but it didn't look like that would be an option.

She rounded the corner into the industrial estate, and immediately saw that things were escalating. Outside the sanctuary, Peter and Judy were in a furious argument with the NLFPC officers. In front of them, three policemen were shouting into their radios. The door of the centre was tight shut, and behind its windows, furniture was piled up.

Behind her, the press were spilling out into the road. Cameras were being set up and aimed. Behind them, the cat people were beginning to file in. one or two, at first, and then, within seconds, hundreds more.

Peter and Judy looked up from their argument and stared at her. She put Christof down on the ground.

"Where have you been?" said Judy.

"I said I had a plan," Laura said simply.

Peter just stared at her and then looked around. She could see what he was thinking. Even to his strangely sideways brain, nothing about the barricades and the police, the cameras and the oddly panting army of Cat People looked anything like a plan.

Laura pulled out her phone and called Samuel.

"The police are coming!" she said, "We haven't got much time."

"I can hold them!" said Samuel.

"I don't want you to hold them." she said.

"You told me to barricade the place!"

"I guess I didn't think you'd do it so well."

"If a job's worth doing - "he said.

"Listen," she whispered into her phone, "I want you to send the cats out."

"All of them?" he said.

"Yes. All of them! There's a cat flap in the front door."

The three confused policemen were discovering quickly that the increasing throng of Cat People were no easier to keep contained than five hundred cats would be, and when actual cats started spilling one by one, out of the front of the building, the crowd surged forward.

Nigela Lawson, and Princess Anne came first, striding stiffly away from each other without a glance back. They were instantly scooped up by an oddly pierced, tattooed girl, and an immensely tall, pale, blond man in a black barrister's gown.

Next came Sherlock. Dark and directed. He eyed the crowd, picked out his student companion, and slunk forward to meet him.

Cats continued to pour from the building. New owners surging in to meet them. The NLFPC officials, and the police tried to put up some kind of protest, but it was no good. Eighty animals and five hundred people, each with their own set of rules of engagement which they would bend to no authority collided in a vortex of colour and passion and fur. Nothing would stop them.

And in the middle of it all, Laura and Christof stood, watching. And the moment the chaotic dance subsided, and the road cleared, the armed response unit arrived.

The heavy police vehicle lurched into the industrial estate, skidded to a halt, and four heavily armoured men leaped out, and took cover behind their vehicle. The leader raised a heavy rifle and aimed it squarely at the door of the sanctuary. His team covered the windows.

Laura whispered into her phone, "You have to come out."

"But - "said Samuel.

"Come out now." she said. She looked behind her at the police marksmen and added, "and Samuel, I'm sorry I got you into this - but just don't do anything stupid."

From behind the door, she could hear the sound of obstacles being removed, furniture being dragged away from the door. The door handle turned, and it slowly opened. Samuel's figure appeared in the shadow of the dark hallway. His hands were clasped in front of him. In them, something black.

"Put it down," Laura yelled at him, "just put it down!"

Behind her, the police sniper raised his gun, and took aim.

"But it's mine now," said Samuel, levelly, "I've decided to keep it."

He stepped out of the shadows.

"Can I?" he said, "Can I keep it?" He raised his arms. In his hands, small and black, the Boston Strangler uncurled himself.

The police marksman lowered his weapon. "Kitten!" He said with military authority, "stand down, it's a kitten."

"I thought..." started Laura.

"What did you think?" said Samuel" "I chucked *that* in the river - what do you think I am? Some kind of idiot?" He cupped his hands around Boston, stroking his head, gently.

Laura paused, then found herself saying, "You know, I think we could go out somewhere one day... If you like."

But Samuel didn't hear her. Samuel had a kitten now.

Printed in Poland
by Amazon Fulfillment
Poland Sp. z o.o., Wrocław